KLONDIKE GOLD RUSH REGION

WE WERE THERE
IN THE
KLONDIKE GOLD RUSH

BENJAMIN APPEL

WE WERE THERE IN THE KLONDIKE GOLD RUSH

HISTORICAL CONSULTANT
Colonel HENRY W. CLARK, U.S.A.R.

ILLUSTRATED BY
IRV DOCKTOR

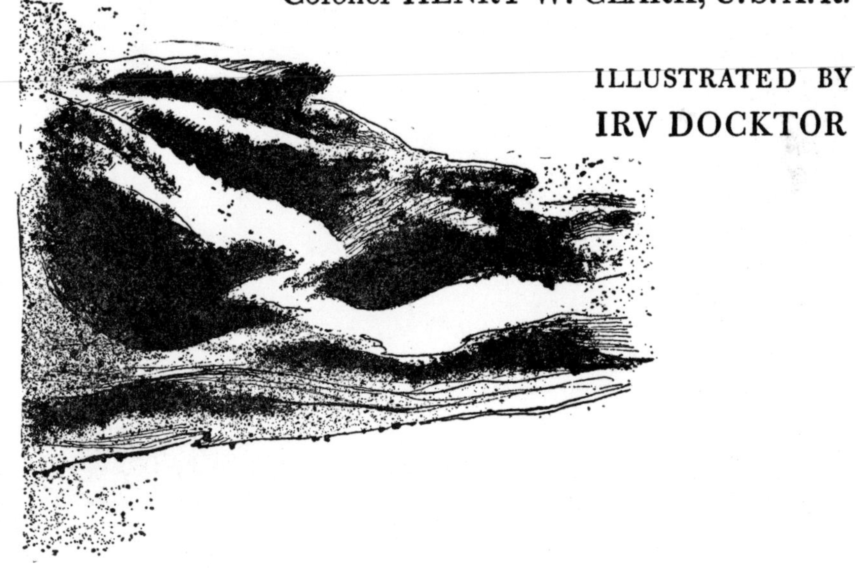

GROSSET & DUNLAP • *Publishers* • NEW YORK

PRINTED IN THE UNITED STATES OF AMERICA
Library of Congress Catalog Card No. 56-5390

We Were There in the Klondike Gold Rush

To
My Two Daughters
CARLA *and* WILLA

Contents

Illustrations

ILLUSTRATIONS

WE WERE THERE
IN THE
KLONDIKE GOLD RUSH

CHAPTER ONE

Gold Fever

THERE'S a river of gold up there!" the boy exclaimed. His blue eyes shone with excitement as he passed his plate to his mother for another helping of Sunday roast chicken.

"River of talk!" Mrs. Murray retorted. She was tired of hearing her family always talking about the gold of Alaska and the Yukon.

The boy, Joe Murray, reached for the salt shaker and lifted it. "Up there," he said, "all they have to do is pick up a rock this size to find gold nuggets big as peas!"

"Joe!" his mother said. "How about some *green* peas with your chicken?"

"Some of those nuggets are big as potatoes!" Joe said, digging his fork into a potato on his sister Anne's plate and holding it up for all of them to see.

It was a big potato, so big that his mother had to smile. Joe's father, Mike Murray, and his uncle Bill Hansen burst out laughing. A gold nugget the size of a potato! Even up in the Yukon, in that year of 1897, nuggets weren't that big! Or were they?

Joe Murray grinned at his family. He was fourteen years old, one year older than his sister Anne, but he seemed twice her size. He had a man's shoulders but a boy's downy cheeks. His blond hair was that of a boy to whom a comb is still an enemy.

"I'd like to find a nugget," Joe said. "Even if it was only a little one."

"So would I!" his sister Anne said eagerly. "If I found a bunch of little ones, I'd string them on some thread and have a necklace!"

Unlike her brother Joe, Anne's hair was black, her eyes dark brown. She was a small girl but she could run as fast as a boy. She liked to play boys' games. In the spring she had made a kite that had flown higher than the kites of any of the boys in their neighborhood.

"So now you want a necklace of gold nuggets," Mrs. Murray said, shaking her head.

"Yes," the girl answered. "And I'd like to dig them out of the ground myself!"

They all laughed at the notion of little Anne Murray as a gold miner!

"They say the Yukon'll beat California in '49," Mike Murray said as if talking to himself. He was a black-haired man, a quiet man, and now his eyes had a faraway look. Mrs. Murray glanced at her husband anxiously. She had seen that look on the faces of the men who thronged the waterfront on Sundays in this city of Seattle where they all lived. The restless men who could only talk of Alaska. Of Alaska and the Yukon and gold!

That year a strange fever had whirled down from the far northern tundras and glaciers, and everybody in Seattle had caught it. The newspapers called it the "gold fever."

Rivers of gold, and gold nuggets the size of potatoes! Gold to make a poor man rich and a rich man richer!

"If there's one half the gold they say there is—" old Bill Hansen said with a sigh. Mrs. Murray's brother was old enough to remember the California gold rush of 1849.

"I don't believe any of these gold stories," Mrs. Murray declared firmly. "There's no proof!"

"The proof'll be here soon," Mike Murray said.

"The steamer *Portland* is due in July. If those stories are true I'm going to Alaska myself!"

Joe's blue eyes opened wide at this announcement. "I'll go with you, Pop!" he cried.

"Me, too, Pop!" his sister Anne echoed.

Their mother had to laugh. "Look at the two gold miners, will you!" she said. "And where'll the money come from to pay all your steamer tickets?"

"I could sell my business," Mike Murray said.

Mrs. Murray stared at her husband as if he

were mad. It had taken him long years to save up the money to buy his carpenter shop.

"I'll stake you, Mike!" old Bill Hansen said. "No need to sell the business."

"I've got forty-six dollars in the bank!" Joe shouted. "Pop, take me! Haven't I been helping you after school?"

"Take Joe!" Mrs. Murray broke in sharply. She pointed at the cat. "And take Puss. There's so much gold up there Puss can scratch up a few nuggets, too!"

They all laughed except Mrs. Murray. Red-faced and worried, she scolded her whole family. "Oh, you cabbageheads! Mike Murray, how can you sit there talking of selling your business? You've worked so hard for it and now that we have this nice comfortable home—"

"It's a nice home," Mike Murray agreed. "But we don't own it. I'd like to build a home of my own. I'd like to send Joe to college—"

"We can save the money to send him!" Mrs. Murray retorted. "Alaska! There's not a year that stories of gold strikes haven't come down from Alaska! And now it's the Yukon and the Klondike! And when the steamer comes in there's nothing to see. Only a few old miners with a little gold dust wrapped up in a handkerchief!"

"We'll see what we'll see when the *Portland* docks," Mike Murray answered her in his quiet way. "If there's gold in the Klondike, it'll be on board the *Portland*."

"You've all got the gold fever!" Mrs. Murray said. "Oh, let's get on with supper before it turns cold!"

All through Seattle in the summer of 1897, the suppers were turning cold as the table talk grew hot. During the winter, exciting letters had been arriving, written by sourdough miners to their relatives. Some of these letters had been printed in the newspapers:

> *"Everyone has gone to the Klondike where the richest strike ever heard of was made last fall."*

The Klondike was a river in the wild Canadian Yukon Territory. The Siwash Indian name for the river was *Thron Diuk* which meant "Hammer Stream." The Indians hammered poles in the mouth of the stream to make traps to catch fish.

Soon the name, Klondike, would be known all over the world.

The steamship *Portland* arrived in Seattle on the morning of July 17th, 1897. At dawn that day the *Portland's* dock was crowded from end to end.

Breathless, Joe Murray and his sister Anne stood up on tiptoe between their father and their uncle Bill. The two men were six-footers, and the boy would be a big man, too, in a few more years.

"Here she comes!" Joe shouted when the *Portland* puffed into sight. He felt that he had called

out with the voice of a giant, for from the throats of all that crowd the same shout had roared:

"Here she comes!"

Old prospectors were in the crowd, men who had hunted for gold in Montana and Arizona. And young high school students who had been reading every book on gold mining they could find. There were jobless men from all over the West and men wearing diamond tiepins.

"Here she comes!" they shouted.

"Here she comes!" Anne shrilled.

The excitement quickened when the Wells Fargo Express Company guards, carrying rifles, marched out on the dock. The crowd pushed forward. Men nudged at each other. "See those rifles!" they said.

"They've got the gold!"

"They must have gold!"

Joe tugged at his father's elbow. "Pop," he pleaded. "If you go, promise you'll take me!"

"Me, too!" his sister Anne cried out.

The *Portland* blew its whistle and came into the dock. "Show us the gold!" the crowd begged.

They squeezed as close as they could get to the gangplank where the Wells Fargo guards had formed two lines of armed men.

"Show us the gold!" Joe and Anne yelled with all the others.

A miner on the *Portland* lifted a leather satchel so heavy that it seemed as if it would tear his arms out of their sockets.

"Hooray for the Klondike!" somebody in the crowd yelled.

Down the gangplank, between the Wells Fargo

guards, marched the bearded miners. They looked like poor men in their ragged shirts and slouch hats. They carried very few personal belongings, but every one of them had a fortune in his fist.

Joe and Anne Murray stared as if hypnotized at the leather satchels, the moosehide sacks, the bundles made from blankets. Gold from the Klondike!

"I'm going," Joe's father whispered as if it were a prayer.

"Pop, take me," the boy said pleadingly.

Old Bill Hansen pounded Mike Murray's broad back. "Every dime I've got in the world's yours!" he promised.

That day, newsboys ran through the streets of Seattle with bundles of the *Post-Intelligencer*. The front page read:

GOLD! GOLD! GOLD! GOLD!

SIXTY-EIGHT RICH MEN ON THE STEAMER PORTLAND

Stacks of Yellow Metal

Some Have $5000, Many Have More, and
a Few Bring Out $100,000 Each

THE STEAMER CARRIES $700,000

The *Portland* had intended to return to Alaska in August. But now it was announced she would leave in five days. The price of a steamer ticket jumped from $200 to $1000.

"There'll be other ships," old Bill Hansen consoled Mike. "Cheaper ships. One thousand dollars fare!"

The *City of Mexico* sailed for Alaska. And the *Al-Ki* and the *Rosalie* and the *State of California.* The huge collier *Willamette* was converted into a transport with one thousand bunks. Freighters and sloops, whalers and pleasure craft, all headed north. It seemed that the whole country had caught the gold fever.

Anne Murray had the gold fever as badly as anyone. She couldn't understand why her brother Joe could go to Alaska and not herself. "Joe is almost a man," Mike Murray told her a dozen times. "You're not strong enough, Annie. And besides I don't want to leave Mother alone."

And when the *Queen* sailed, among the four hundred gold-rushers were the two Murrays. Joe, standing beside his father, waved good-by to his mother and Anne and his uncle Bill. The boy could hardly believe that he, Joe Murray, was bound for the Klondike. But down below on the dock, his mother's face was getting smaller and smaller, and his sister's face, and his uncle's face—the faces of home.

"Joe, you'll remember to wear your long winter underwear," his mother called tearfully. "Take care of each other."

"Joe," his sister reminded him, "don't forget you promised to write me every day."

"Bring back the gold!" his uncle shouted. "Bring back the gold!"

CHAPTER TWO

"Klondike or Bust!"

YOU'RE in a man's world now," Mike Murray said to his son when they sat down to their first meal on board the *Queen*.

At the long tables, the *Queen's* passengers were talking in excited voices. "I've got weak lungs," a thin man was saying. "But I figure I might better die making a fortune than die broke in Kansas where I come from."

"The gold's lying on the bottom of the creeks like a long, shiny ribbon," another man said, as positively as if he had just seen it himself.

Mike Murray shook his head with a wondering sort of pity. "Joe, they're forgetting it's a terrible wilderness up there. Sometimes I say to myself, 'Mike, the devil must have got into you to take your own flesh and blood into a wilderness like that.' "

Dreamy-eyed, the boy listened to his father. He

wouldn't have been anywhere in the world but on the *Queen,* bound for the Klondike gold creeks.

It was a five-day voyage to the *Queen's* destination, Dyea, on Alaskan soil. As the days passed, the long-legged, blue-eyed boy met all kinds of men. Farmers and college professors and soldiers. There was even a medium from Chicago, a man who claimed he could talk to the dead. Other mediums in his home city had raised the money, "grubstaked" him, so he could travel to the Klondike and find gold. "I'll receive messages from the spirit world," he explained to Joe. "They'll tell me the best place to dig."

Another man had put money in a company called the Arctic Gopher Company. "They'll breed Arctic gophers," he told Joe and his father. "When the ground's so frozen you can't dent it with a pick, I'll let my gophers do the digging for me."

"We're green as grass," Mike Murray said later to his son. "Nothing but tenderfeet—*cheechakos,* they'll call us in the Klondike. But compared to that gopher miner we're a pair of wise old sourdoughs."

Most of the men on the *Queen* were going up to the Klondike in teams of two or three. It was the

It was a five-day voyage

kind of wild, desolate country where a man had to have a partner. They would have to endure seven long, dreary months of winter, and the temperature would drop to forty and fifty degrees below zero. Down in the hold of the ship was their gear, a thousand pounds to a man, everything to keep a man for a year. Food and clothing and tools and medicine.

On the third morning out of Seattle, Joe got up before breakfast time. He wrote a letter to his sister Anne, telling her about the men on board ship. The letter would be posted from Dyea.

Joe walked up the steps to the deck. The *Queen* was threading her way through the Inland Passage—a sea-water route between the rugged coast and mountainous islands. Forests of evergreens grew on the lower slopes of the mountains. The icy tongues of glaciers licked out among the masses of dark green trees.

"Boo!" somebody called behind Joe.

Joe turned, startled. Winking at him was a man wearing a black derby and a fancy jacket. But instead of shoes, he had Indian moccasins on his feet.

"Let's feel your muscle," the man said, grabbing at Joe's arm.

Joe pulled away, and the man took off his hat and laughed. "You going to fill your diaper with gold?" he asked.

"Never mind, mister!" Joe said angrily. "Leave me alone!"

"Diamond Jack Munson is the name," the man introduced himself. "Some dig for gold with their muscle and some dig with their brains." Diamond Jack smiled, and his broad face with its black mustache was like a clown's. But no clown ever had such sharp eyes. He tapped his temple and said, "Here's where I carry my shovel."

"How do you dig for gold that way?" Joe asked.

"Come here and I'll show you," Diamond Jack said. He led Joe over to a sheltered part of the deck. He took three walnut half shells out of his pocket and placed them down on top of a box of cargo. "Sonny, this is the game of the nuts!" he announced. "Keep your eye steady, sonny, while I take this pea out of my pocket and demonstrate that the hand is quicker than the eye. Do you see this pea, sonny?"

Joe was smiling now. There was something about Diamond Jack that reminded him of a barker at a circus. "Sure, I see it," Joe said.

"Ah, what confidence!" Diamond Jack smiled. "He sees it, he says. Ah, what I would give to be young again! What's the Chilkoot Pass to innocent youth? What's the White Horse Rapids where many a good man's drowned trying to get to the gold creeks? Nothing but a little green pea. Listen, *cheechako!* I'm going to bet you the gold mine you're sure to find against one million dollars in cash that my hand is quicker than your young and innocent blue eyes."

He put the pea down on the box and began moving the walnut half shells, covering the pea, uncovering it. Faster and faster! "Remember, my young friend. You're betting your gold mine that you can tell me where the pea is. Now, where is it?"

"Here," Joe said, and he picked up the shell on the far left.

The pea wasn't there. Diamond Jack laughed and lifted up the shell in the middle. It, too, was empty. "By process of elimination," he announced, "it must be here."

He picked up the last shell, revealing the pea. "Yes," Diamond Jack said. "If the captain of this ship wasn't such a bluenose I could have won all the gear in the hold. And a good thing it would've been, too. Then none of you *cheechakos* would have to carry a thousand pounds of stuff up the Chilkoot Pass. Suppose we forget our bet and push some breakfast grub into our faces?"

The gambler took a liking for the boy. Maybe because Joe was such a good listener. They were together often during the rest of the passage.

On the fifth day out of Seattle, the *Queen* entered Lynn Canal. After six hours on the gray waters of the canal, Dyea loomed into sight. Joe looked at a jumble of shacks and tents and corrals. It was a frontier town he saw on the beach, hemmed in by mountains. A mile up the beach were the cedar slab huts of the Chilkoot Indians.

Civilization—such as it was—was limited to the flatland. The wilderness, like a great dark hand, seemed to reach down from the mountains, threatening to push both white man and red man into the sea.

The joy of arrival didn't last long. The captain of the *Queen* spoke through a megaphone to the four hundred passengers.

"Gentlemen," the captain said, "there is no wharf at Dyea. Scows will put you and your freight ashore just as fast as it can be done. When the tide turns I must take my ship out of here!"

In the next hour the orderly ship changed into a warehouse. Bags of flour, boxes of dried fruit, kegs of nails were hauled up out of the hold and transferred to the scows. Everybody was working, passengers as well as crew.

Mike Murray grabbed a sack from Joe's shoulder. "You rest a minute, Joe," he said.

Joe reeled over to the rail and watched the scows. Indian dugouts—long logs shaped into roughhewn craft—were also carrying the miners' outfits into Dyea, while floating in on the tide were drums of kerosene that had been heaved overboard. And in the icy water, the horses and sled dogs brought from Seattle by the *Queen* were swimming for shore.

"Hey, gold miner!" Diamond Jack yelled to Joe from a dugout. "If you get into trouble, I'll be at the New York Kitchen!"

When Joe and his father jumped ashore from one of the scows, they felt as if they

had come to a madhouse. Along the muddy beach of the canal, the mixed-up outfits of the *Queen's* four hundred passengers were piled high in a wall of boxes and sacks. Frantic, shouting men were digging into the wall as the tide sucked in closer and closer.

"That's my stove!" somebody screamed. "Keep your hands off or I'll belt you one!"

Men splashed knee-deep in the water, shouting and arguing, as they hunted for their possessions. "The tide's reached our flour!" another man hollered at his partner.

"Ain't there no Indians we can hire?"

"There's only the Dyea thieves!"

For a second Joe and his father stood still, stunned. Then Mike Murray yelled at his son. "Joe, come on!"

Silently, they darted in among the swarming men, searching for their supplies. They lugged sacks of flour up to the beach. Once, Joe was almost sure he saw some of the Dyea men going off with a box of their tools.

"Pop!" he cried. "They're taking our gear!"

"We've got to take our chances like the rest," his father muttered bitterly. "There's no police in Dyea."

Later that day, the two Murrays sat inside the tent they had retrieved and pitched on the beach. They peered gloomily through the open flap at the remains of their outfit.

"Joe," his father said at last, "we've got to talk

this over like two men, not like I'm your father. We've lost most of our hardware. What wasn't stolen or washed away in the tide is missing and we'll never see it again."

"We saved most of our grub," Joe said.

"Joe," Mike Murray said, sighing and shaking his head, "it's a bad beginning. It's 'Klondike or bust' all right."

"Pop," Joe said, trying to cheer his father, "we're not the only ones who lost some of our gear."

"It's a long way to Dawson City," Mike Murray went on. "The Chilkoot Pass! Six hundred miles of rough water!"

"Pop, what we ought to do is go into Dyea and see if we can hire some Indians to help us over the Chilkoot Pass," Joe said. "That's what Diamond Jack said we should do."

The father was silent for a few seconds, his eyes fixed intently on his son. Then his solemn face split into a wide, slow grin. "Joe," he said, "you're the best partner a man could have."

CHAPTER THREE

Poor Man's Pass

MIKE MURRAY asked the men in the next tent to keep an eye on their things. Then he and Joe walked up the beach, skirting the tents and heaps of supplies belonging to the gold-rushers.

"Can we trust them, Pop?" the boy asked anxiously.

"Yes. They're gold-rushers like us. Not Dyea thieves."

Dyea hadn't looked like much of a place from the deck of the ship. It was even more raw and ugly close at hand. Its single street was ankle deep in mud, and through it sloshed the endless crowd who had come off the ships in Lynn Canal. The skinniest horses Joe had ever seen pulled heavily loaded wagons, and shoeless, starved horses wandered around the town like stray cats. Their ribs showed like pieces of stone.

"Poor horses," Joe said with tears in his eyes.

A bearded man passing by heard him. "Hay costs two hundred dollars a ton in Dyea," the man said. "They feed 'em on packing straw, work the animals almost to death, and turn 'em loose. That's Dyea for you!"

"I guess you couldn't hire a pack horse?" Mike Murray asked doubtfully.

"To get you up the Chilkoot Pass?" The man laughed bitterly. "Ain't ten horses left alive. If you're thinkin' of Injuns, forget them too."

"Why?" Joe's father asked.

"Those Injuns're too rich to work," the man said. "Used to charge five cents a pound. The price is thirty cents now. You better pack your own truck up the Chilkoot. It's the poor man's pass anyhow!"

"I don't see you packing your own truck," Mike Murray said.

"No, you don't," the man replied. "My partner was shot dead in an argument the day we came. One of these days I'll get the courage to go home and tell his wife. He was my own brother, he was."

"I'm sorry," Joe's father said quickly.

Without another word the man walked away

from them. Mike Murray glanced at Joe but said nothing. The father's dark brown eyes did the talking for him now. His eyes were full of pity.

In the middle of the street they found the New York Kitchen and asked for Diamond Jack Munson. The proprietor directed them to the Palace Hotel. It was a hotel under canvas, a tent hotel, and inside, on rows of cots, men were sleeping or talking. Diamond Jack waved at Joe and his father. "Hello, you two *cheechakos,*" he greeted them.

He stepped forward and they sat down on a log bench. Diamond Jack gave Mike Murray a cigar. "Cost a dollar apiece in Dyea," he boasted. "Smoke up, man, and you won't look so sad."

"Thanks," Mike Murray said. "I'll save it for the time when I feel like celebrating."

They told Diamond Jack everything that had happened. When they were done, Diamond Jack said, "I'll try and get you some Indians. Got any money?"

"Yes," Mike Murray said, patting the money belt he wore under his shirt.

"Don't do that!" Diamond Jack hissed. "Let's walk."

Out on the muddy street, Diamond Jack said

thoughtfully, "You don't want to buy tools in Dyea. Buy them when you get to Dawson City. They'll charge you more in Dawson City but it'll be worth it. The less you have to carry up the Chilkoot Pass the better. The main thing you've got to worry about is time."

"Winter starts early here," Joe's father said, nodding.

"It's not only that," Diamond Jack said. "The longer you're on the trail the less chance you got for a gold claim. Every sourdough from Alaska is up there in the Klondike. Thousands of *cheechakos* are there or on the way."

"You mean we mightn't get to the Klondike in time to stake a claim?" Mike Murray asked, worried.

"That's right," Diamond Jack said. "You've got to hustle." He winked at Joe. "Want to stay here and work for me? Plenty of good *cheechako* gold in Dyea. I'm going to do a little 'digging' right here before I come up to Dawson City."

Two days later Diamond Jack brought a family of Chilkoots over to where Joe and his father were camping on the beach. "This is Chief Charlie," Diamond Jack said, nodding at a round-faced Indian. "It'll cost you forty cents a pound for your gear. Pay him now."

Mike Murray groaned. "That's four hundred dollars for the thousand pounds of gear we've got."

"Time's the thing to worry about," Diamond Jack said. He grinned at Joe. "If your old man ever forgets, you remind him." He dug his hand into his pocket and pulled out a pair of caribou mittens which he tossed to the boy. "That's for digging gold when it's twenty below zero."

"Thanks!" The boy beamed with pleasure.

"Now, before you take down your tent," Diamond Jack said, "let's go inside for a powwow."

Joe and his father were puzzled, but they followed Diamond Jack into the tent. The gambler closed the flaps and said, "Mike, I'll bet you ten to one you're still carrying your money in your belt."

"What's wrong with that?" Mike Murray asked.

"There've been a lot of robberies on the trail to the Pass," Diamond Jack said. "Keep a little money in your belt. If you're held up, say that's all you got. The rest of your money, stick in your boots. Divide it up between you! Do it now!"

Joe and his father pulled off their boots, and as they placed the bills inside, Diamond Jack laughed. "You'll walk on money up the Chilkoot," he said.

Joe laced his boots and said, "I'll be walking on two thousand dollars."

"I've got about the same," his father murmured. "That money is about all of your uncle's savings, Joe."

"You'll bring Uncle back a bootful of gold dust," Diamond Jack said.

They went outside, and Mike Murray paid Chief Charlie four hundred dollars. Diamond Jack shook hands with the boy and his father. "Good luck," he said. "See you in Dawson City."

Soon they were ready to hit the trail. Every Indian had a pack. Chief Charlie was weighed down with a hundred-pound flour sack and a fifty-pound corn sack. His squaw carried close to a hundred pounds. Their four children and their two dogs all were loaded.

"We're not Indians," Mike Murray said to Joe. "But we'll have to pitch in. I'll give you about seventy pounds, Joe. And I'll match Chief Charlie."

Joe smiled. "If Annie were here, she'd be surprised at how much those little Indians can carry."

The trail first led to the Dyea River where the Indians put most of the outfit into a canoe. Chief Charlie and his oldest son paddled the canoe upstream. The river was narrow, not more than fifty yards wide. The wet, slippery trail crossed from side to side. The squaw, her three other children, and the two dogs still were bent under packs on the trail. But Joe's seventy pounds was in the canoe. Now with only a rifle in his fist, he felt light as a bubble.

Ahead was the winding trail and other Dawson City-bound gold-rushers moving slowly like human pack mules. Behind them, Joe heard the voices of still other gold-rushers. He glanced at the silent Chilkoots and thought how lucky he and his father were to have Indians to help them.

The sun glittered on the river. The gorge that the Dyea River had cut was dark with birch and spruce and cottonwood. When they stopped for lunch, Joe picked wild berries. Among the wild flowers, salmon berries and huckleberries grew big and plump.

"It's a short summer in the North," Joe's father said as he tossed a handful of ripe huckleberries into his mouth.

The Indians grinned at the two whites. Chief

Charlie opened up a sealskin pouch from which he removed long strips of smoked salmon. The squaw boiled tea in an old tomato can.

Suddenly, out of the woods on the east side of the trail, three bearded men broke out like frightened deer. But their faces were as hard as the rifles they aimed at Joe and his father.

"We want your money!" their leader cried.

Another of the band spoke to the Chilkoots in their own language. The Indians listened, still as stones. Joe watched his father unbutton his shirt and unstrap the money belt.

The leader snatched the belt and opened the pockets. His face flushed with anger. "Thirty dollars!" he growled.

"We spent our last money getting here," Mike Murray said.

"Search the boy!" the leader ordered.

One of the men ripped Joe's shirt open to see if he had a money belt strapped around his waist. Joe felt a terrible temptation to look down at his boots. Inside each boot was a thousand dollars! But he kept his eyes on his father's expressionless face.

"Cheechakos!" the leader snarled. And as suddenly as they had come they melted away among

the trees. They had made no attempt to rob the Indians. Chief Charlie explained why to Joe's father. "Takum Chilkoot money, we findum Dyea." He lifted his hands as if holding an imaginary rifle. "Thlink!" he imitated rifle fire. "Thlink!"

"They call Chilkoot Pass the Poor Man's Pass," Mike Murray said to his son. "If it hadn't been for Diamond Jack we'd be poor all right."

The next day they reached Sheep Camp, the six Indians and the two Murrays all under heavy loads. For the trail no longer bordered the Dyea River. A flat meadow

stretched before them with one exit—the Pass. There were no woods here. Glaciers locked the meadow in on all sides. And everywhere the gold-rushers were camped, resting their aching bones before the real work of climbing the Chilkoot.

"You're lucky you've got Indians," one of the campers said to Mike Murray, who was frying bacon and boiling coffee at their fire.

"We lost half our outfit on the beach," Joe's father said. "But I guess we're lucky at that—"

His voice was drowned out as a thunderous roar like cannon fire exploded in the north. When the echoes died away, the camper grinned and pointed to a glacier of blue ice that reached down to the valley floor from a ledge two thousand feet above them.

"They never sleep," the camper explained. "Always grinding down the mountains, those glaciers."

It took the rest of the day to bring their gear to the bottom of the Chilkoot Pass. Joe stared up at the trail which seemed to have sprouted wings, winding up to a cliff of sliding rock. "That's Chilkoot Glacier," his father said. "Chief Charlie thinks it'll take us six hours to climb. We'll try it in the morning."

That night Joe slept restlessly. His whole body ached from the pack he had lugged all day long. In the stillness of the night, the never-resting glaciers snapped and crashed and roared. He dreamed of the robbers. He dreamed that the robbers were stealing the letters he had written home to his sister Anne.

The Alaskan summer sun that had sunk at nine o'clock that night showed itself again at four in the morning. Joe turned over, sleeping on his face.

At four-thirty they all awoke, eating a hurried breakfast. The youngest Indian child was left with the two dogs. Chief Charlie said, "Dog no likum Chilkoot."

Joe tilted his head back and looked up at the cliff. He thought he didn't like the Chilkoot either.

Under their heavy packs, Chief Charlie in the lead, the party entered the defile. Above their heads, a line of men, each man weighed down under a load, were creeping up the trail.

"Joe, I'll go last," his father said pantingly. "If you—if you slip, I'll—I'll catch you."

The trail suddenly had seemed to stand on end. Joe's pack felt as if it had doubled its weight. The straps burned his shoulders as he inched up to the huge boulders an early gold-rusher had christened the Stone Houses. The wind rushed out of the boy's lungs. His strength began to fail. "O God," he prayed, "please don't let me get tired so quick."

Up, up, he forced himself, clinging with his hands and feet to the steep, stony trail. His pack seemed to change into an enemy that wanted to tear him loose from his precarious hand-holds. He gritted his teeth and groped for the next stony knob above him . . .

After three hours they stopped to eat. Joe could hardly chew the half-cooked beans his father passed to him. The beans were pinkish inside, and Mike Murray grimaced. "Now I know why they call these beans Alaska strawberries! Joe, we'll have a good meal tonight when we're over the divide. How do you feel, son?"

Joe tried to smile as his tired jaws champed slowly on the half-raw beans. He glanced at the silent Indians eating their smoked salmon. Mike Murray gave Joe a tin cup of coffee. The boy gulped the hot stuff down and felt a little better. But when he looked at the perpendicular wall of blue ice on his left, at the broken rocks littering the slope on his right, his stomach tightened. Far

They were like flies glued to the cliff

above him, and below, he could see other gold-rushers eating. They were all like flies glued to the cliff.

His exhausted body shivered when Chief Charlie strapped his pack onto his back. He felt he couldn't go another step. But when the line of climbers began to move he moved with them. He wondered if he'd stumble or fall. If he did he might knock his father down the cliff with him and kill them both!

The trail became steeper near the top. Joe's heart was pounding as he zigzagged from hold to hold. As if in a dream he followed the Chilkoots above him to the base of what seemed like a second cliff. The sun had darkened and the air was gray, and in this grayness he was like a sleepwalker.

Out of nowhere a wind roared. The human flies on the cliff froze to their holds. Nobody was climbing now. Mike Murray shouted up to Joe, "Hold on, son, till it blows over!"

It was one of the sudden storms that summer and winter whipped around the Chilkoot Pass.

The grayness thickened into a heavy fog. To Joe, the whole world had shrunk to a few yards of dimly seen rock. He shuddered as the wind howled. Sleet whipped into his face and he could no longer see the Indians above him or his father below. He was alone with the heavy pack that was trying to pull him down into death. A gray death, gray as the fog!

He held on desperately until the storm disappeared. It vanished as quickly as the three holdup men of two days ago. Again the line began to move, keeping along the base of the cliff. And almost before Joe knew it, he was following their Indians across the divide.

The sky was blue and serene. On top of the Pass, the redcoated Canadian Mounties were waiting to inspect the gear of the gold-rushing Americans.

CHAPTER FOUR

Rough Water

LAKE LINDERMAN, ten miles from the Chilkoot Pass, was the first of many water hurdles between the gold-rushers and the gold creeks six hundred miles to the north.

Everywhere on the lake men were building the boats to transport them and their outfits to Dawson City on the faraway Yukon River. Everywhere the tap-tap of hammers sounded like iron woodpeckers.

"Time!" the boat builders all said. "Time's worth its weight in gold!"

For although it was August, with daylight eighteen hours a day, the northern winter could begin in five or six weeks. A September blizzard could howl down from the Arctic. By October, at the latest, the lakes and the rivers would be frozen solid.

There was a sawmill at Lake Linderman, but the owner charged seventy-five dollars for a boat. Mike Murray shook his head stubbornly. "We've got to stretch every nickel now," he said to his son. "We've got to buy tools and mining equipment in Dawson City. And a dog team when the snows come. I'll talk to some of these men who don't know a whipsaw from a whip." As a carpenter who knew how to use tools, Mike Murray enjoyed this little joke.

He made a bargain with two Chicago men called Tom Conkle and Roy Britt. "We lost our tools at Dyea," he said to them. "I'm a first-class carpenter, and if you're willing I will show you how to build a sailboat that'll take us all to Dawson City."

They cut down a spruce and sawed out the lumber. "We saw wood," Tom Conkle grinned. "And the mosquitoes saw us." He was a red-haired man of forty who had been a bank clerk in Chicago where his partner Roy Britt had been a bookkeeper.

Clouds of mosquitoes hovered like smoke in the air. The three men and the boy made themselves masks of mosquito netting to protect their eyes and faces. They only took them off at meals when they ate in the thick smoke of their smudge fires.

"That's why you can't find a moose," a passing hunter complained. "All the game's run up to the snow line to get away from the skeeters."

In a week they had their boat built. Tom Conkle wanted to call the boat *Klondike or Bust*. His partner suggested they call the boat after President McKinley. But Mike Murray said, "Let Joe christen her."

The boy scratched his blond thatch of hair. "Pop, Annie wanted to come with us," he said. "Let's call her the *Annie*."

Down nine-mile Lake Linderman, the *Annie* sailed with its four passengers and their outfits. The wind bellied out the canvas sail Joe's father had rigged.

At the tail end of the lake, they portaged boat and gear to the head of thirty-mile Lake Bennett. It was back-breaking work. They had to carry every pound of their supplies. Mosquitoes swarmed at them. The sun burned so fiercely that Joe couldn't imagine winter.

"Here we go!" his father shouted with joy as once more they pushed off into the water.

"These lakes are fine," the bookkeeper Roy

Britt said. "It's the river rapids that worry me. We have Miles Canyon ahead of us, and the Squaw Whirlpool, and the White Horse Rapids."

"We'll worry about the rapids when we get to them," Mike Murray said cheerfully. "Isn't that right, son?"

"Yes, Pop," the boy said.

"If we lose our boat," Roy Britt said glumly, "we'll never get to Dawson City."

Dark purple canyons arose from the lake's white beaches. In the distance, red mountains of iron ore were crowned with ice. Blue glaciers glinted between the trees, and all these colors were reflected in the still waters.

A wind blew up and they pulled in their oars and sailed along lazily. "They say nobody before ever thought there was gold in the Klondike," Tom Conkle said. "A country all moss and mud and moose pastures."

The wind rippled through the black hair of Joe's father. The big man's dark eyes were quiet and thoughtful. "It took George Carmack and his two Indian brothers-in-law to find gold on Rabbit Creek last year," he said.

"That creek's called the Bonanza now," Tom

Conkle said and smiled. "Think we *cheechakos* will find a bonanza?"

"So far we've only found plenty of hard work," Mike Murray said.

"Maybe we'll find a fortune in gold! A bonanza of our own!" Tom Conkle said.

Whenever they passed another party of gold-rushers, Joe shouted over, "What's the name of your boat?"

Some of the boats were named after the states of the Union. Others were named after luck. There was the *Golden Horseshoe* and the *Lucky Star*. Every kind of a boat was racing down Lake Bennett, wherries and rafts and catboats—all bound for the gold creeks.

The four passengers of the *Annie* only went ashore to eat. Night and day they rowed and sailed down the lake. They reached the riverway leading into the next lake, Tagish Lake. Tagish Lake and twenty-mile Mud Lake! One by one, the water miles dropped behind the stern of the *Annie*.

"We'll be in the rapids soon," Roy Britt said nervously. "My hands sweat when I think of the men who have drowned in them."

The next day they were on the swift Miles River

that emptied out of Mud Lake. They didn't have to use their oars now. The two Chicago men sat stiff and dry-lipped as the *Annie* streaked between the banks.

"Joe, keep a sharp lookout!" his father yelled from the stern where he sat at the rudder.

In the bow Joe stared ahead at the leaping water. Suddenly the river seemed to end against a stone wall. "Pop!" he shouted. "There's no more river!"

"Oh, oh!" Roy Britt moaned.

"That's a bend!" Mike Murray said, pushing over the rudder.

At Fifty-Mile they beached the *Annie* and stepped ashore. Back at Lake Linderman they had been warned to go ashore first before trying to run the rapids of Miles Canyon.

They climbed to the top of the canyon's hundred-foot basalt walls. Eight or nine men from other boats were standing there, talking in low voices and peering down at the roaring river. Some of the men cut a small pine and tossed it into the river. Joe stared as the tree vanished, sucked out of sight by the white water.

"You got a mile of that," one of the men said. "If you make it, there's the Squaw to get through. And the White Horse Rapids after the Squaw."

"Too many men've drowned down there," another gold-rusher muttered.

Roy Britt was trembling. When they returned to the *Annie*, he refused to step into the boat. It took almost an hour to change his mind.

"You left Chicago to find gold," Tom Conkle said over and over again. "You're not going to find it unless we get to the Klondike."

"An old riverman back at Linderman told me how to handle the boat," Mike Murray said to Roy Britt. "Before we hit the Squaw I'll holler, 'Row!'

and when I do you'll all row as hard as you can. That's all there is to it."

At last they all stepped into the *Annie.* Joe's eyes darted to a slab of wood lying on the bottom of the boat. On that slab his father had written down their names in pencil and the date. Joe remembered what his father had said: "That's our gravestone if we don't make it."

That slab was enough to scare the daylight out of anybody, Joe thought. He couldn't blame Roy Britt for being so worried. He was, himself.

Then all thought spilled out of the boy's mind as the *Annie* leaped forward in the furious current. The canyon walls slid before his eyes and the sound of the river drummed against his ears. He felt himself falling through space as the river dropped in its mad run. He gasped at the sight of a capsized boat ahead of them, glancing at his father in the stern, his hands on the rudder.

Faster and faster the *Annie* shot between the walls of the canyon like a bullet made of wood aimed at the whirlpool ahead of them—the dreaded Squaw. If they were pulled into the whirlpool they would spin in circles until the *Annie* broke apart or was smashed.

Joe sat numbly at his oar, wondering when his father would give the signal to row. At last it came.

"Row ashore!" Mike Murray boomed. "Row, boys!"

Joe and the two Chicago men dug their oars into the torrent. They pulled with all their might while Mike Murray at the rudder urged them on like a coxswain in a shell. "Row! Row! Row!"

It had all happened so swiftly, Joe felt as if he were dreaming. But there was the *Annie* safe on the bank below the whirlpool. There was Roy, who had jumped out of the boat, lying on the ground like a drowned man. There was red-haired Tom sprawled, half collapsed, in the boat. Only his father sat upright, his dark brown eyes steady.

It took a long time before they could persuade Roy Britt to get into the *Annie* again. "Those White Horse Rapids are sure death," he muttered over and over.

Joe's father unpacked a box and from a pile of socks he extracted a single cigar, the one Diamond Jack had given him at Dyea. "Roy," he said, "I was saving this for the time when I found a gold mine. It's a dollar cigar, Roy. Smoke it."

They shoved off into the river. Behind them

they heard yells. Joe turned. His eyes filled with tears. Caught in the Squaw, a boat of Klondikers was spinning round and round in a doomed circle. No one could help them, Joe knew. He bit on his lips to keep from sobbing.

And again all thoughts emptied out of the boy's head.

The channel of the river had narrowed to twenty feet and, for a quarter of a mile, the water was crazy wild. Waves tossed and jumped, the spray leaping fifteen and twenty feet high like racing white horses. The galloping spray drenched Joe from head to foot. He choked as he breathed in the wet, saturated air. Before him, white water was boiling on the boulders. He saw boats ahead of the *Annie,* plunging down the rapids. How could they escape hitting those boats, he wondered. Or the boulders!

When he heard his father saying, "We made it, thank God!" Joe couldn't believe his own ears.

The river was still foamy white, but it was much calmer here. They were safe, Joe realized slowly. Behind them were the White Horse Rapids and the Squaw and Miles Canyon. Ahead of them was Lake LaBerge.

It would be smooth sailing down Lake LaBerge

and the Thirty-Mile River, long, carefree, sunny days until they reached the great Yukon River. There they would travel fifty miles a day, day after day, until they saw the British Union Jacks waving from the cabins of Dawson City.

And outside of Dawson City were the gold creeks they had endured so many perils and hardships to find—the gold creeks of the Klondike.

CHAPTER FIVE

"You Came Too Late!"

DAWSON CITY in September, 1897, was booming with gold-rushers. Some had taken the Jack Dalton trail which, although an easy one, was unpopular. There was too much walking—three hundred and fifty miles of it. Others had come in style, by steamer to St. Michael on the northwestern coast of Alaska. There they had transferred to the river boats, to chug another fifteen hundred miles up the Yukon to Dawson City. But most of the gold-rushers had come in over the Chilkoot Pass from Dyea or the White Pass from Skagway.

When the four passengers of the *Annie* arrived in Dawson City, they hurried to the Gold Commissioner's office. The Canadian clerk listened to their eager questions, then said: "There are few creeks left that haven't been staked. You men came too late!"

Wooden stakes were used by the gold-rushers to mark off their claims. Canadian Mining Law stated that every claim had to be staked first before it could be legally recorded.

They heard the same story everywhere. They had come too late! Walking down Dawson City's main street, Front Street, they looked dejectedly at the boats of the gold-rushers lined up for two miles on the Yukon River, clear over to Moosehide Hill. How could there be gold mines for so many people!

"The old-timers got all the best claims!" a sour-faced *cheechako* said in answer to Mike Murray's worried questions.

Crowds of men milled up and down the muddy main street, or loitered in front of the combination saloon-gambling-dance halls. Some of the disappointed gold-rushers were leaving while they could. Everybody spoke of what a bad winter it was sure to be. There wasn't enough food in Dawson City. The price of a sack of flour had jumped to two hundred and fifty dollars. A meal in a Front Street restaurant cost seven dollars. There would be starvation and scurvy once the snows fell!

"Break your heart getting here," redheaded

Tom Conkle muttered, "and there's nothing."

"I'm going back to Chicago," Roy Britt said.

Joe glanced at his father's sad face. He wished he could do or say something to cheer him up. But what was there to do?

"Mike, we better split up," Tom Conkle said. "Roy is going home and I don't know what I'll do. You're a fine man, Mike. You can have our half of the *Annie*."

"Thanks," Mike Murray said. "The boy and I will have a place to sleep anyway."

They shook hands and parted. The father put his arm around his son's shoulders and said, "Here we are, Joe. The original two partners."

Mike Murray sighed and stared up Front Street. Redcoated Mounties walked by. Bearded sourdough miners in from the creeks hooted and shouted, their pokes full of gold dust. Indians smelling of salmon circled the knots of idling *cheechakos*. In the gutter a team of dogs pulled a cart with a pine coffin.

"Joe," the dark-haired big man said, "No sense hanging around here. We'll only get to feeling sorry for ourselves. Let's go and see what we can see."

The boy grinned, and his father looking at him had to smile.

They hired a teamster to bring their outfit into a warehouse on Front Street. Then they bought two gold pans, a shovel, and a pick in one of the tent-stores. The pans would be used to wash the gold out of the creek gravel and mud.

The proprietor fingered their paper money. "*Cheechako* money," he said as if it were worth-

less. In all the stores there were gold scales to weigh the gold dust used by the sourdoughs to pay for their purchases.

Toward noon, the two Murrays crossed to the south bank of the Klondike River which emptied into the broad Yukon River. The wet, slippery trail to the gold creeks began here.

They hadn't gone a mile when a dog team approached, each dog carrying a heavy sack tied to its body.

"Joe!" the older Murray said. "Know what's inside those sacks?"

"Clear the trail!" one of the drivers shouted. There were twenty dogs in the team and three drivers.

"How much gold in one of those sacks?" Joe's father asked the driver.

"Twenty to thirty pounds." The driver studied the father and son. "This train's hauling a hundred thousand dollars in gold dust. Wish it was mine," he added.

"I guess you came too late, like us," Mike Murray said.

"Tell you about it some other time!" the driver grinned. "Clear the trail, you *cheechakos!*"

Other gold trains passed the two Murrays. All summer long, twenty-four hours a day, the gold trains were on the trail, bringing in the dust from the creeks.

When the two Murrays reached the famous Bonanza Creek where George Carmack and his two Indian brothers-in-law had first discovered gold to start the Klondike gold rush, Joe gazed about him wide-eyed. He saw a beehive of sluices and dams, ash dumps and prospect holes. The pay-streak was always deep underground and to find it, prospect holes had to be sunk. Everywhere on their claims, miners were busy washing out the winter's diggings. They shoveled the gold-laden gravel into the sluices and let the water in to wash out the pay dirt. Or holding gold pans, their eyes fixed like hypnotized men, they shook the pans, fascinated by the magic yellow stuff they uncovered.

It was all exciting to Joe. Yet he felt a little disappointed. Perhaps he had expected a mining camp to be bright as a circus. These ragged, bearded miners looked like tramps, their log cabins like pigsties put down helter-skelter in a wasteland of stumps. Once this country had been covered

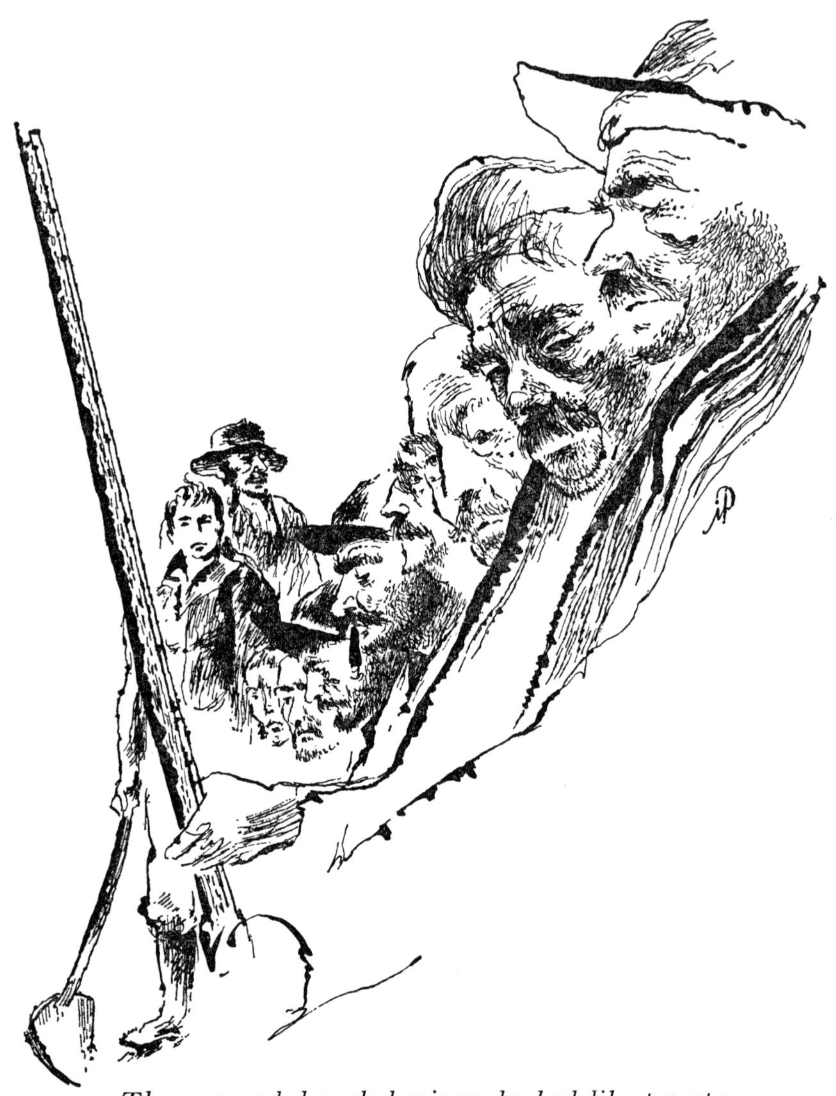

These ragged, bearded miners looked like tramps

with timber and russet-colored moss. Now the only living plants were tufts of coarse grass and the devil-club bushes whose thorns and spiked leaves could cut through leather.

"Getting much gold?" Mike Murray asked two miners at a sluice.

They didn't answer but kept on shoveling the gravel in as if someone were standing over them with a shotgun. Nearly everyone was too busy to spare a word for a couple of *cheechakos*.

"We sure would be grateful for some advice," Mike Murray said to a man with a bandaged arm, on a claim where fifteen men were at work.

"You don't want advice," the man replied. "You want a claim! Why don't you dig a hole in the Klondike River?"

It was a standard joke among the sourdough miners. The Klondike River was too deep and too turbulent for gold mining.

The two Murrays moved on. The trail edged the bogs and twisted in and out among the miners' camps. It circled dumps of waste dirt and pay dirt. The pay dirt had come out of the prospect holes that had hit the rich paystreak.

For three days, Mike Murray and Joe investigated the gold creeks. The talk back in Dawson City had not been exaggerated. The Bonanza was staked to the last inch. On the fifteen miles of Eldorado Creek, there wasn't a single spot where they could dip an exploratory gold pan. It was all claimed.

Nights, they slept in some miner's cabin. The same men who wouldn't give them a civil word during the working day relaxed when the sun sank.

"I'll give you some advice," a miner named Larry Arp said to them one evening. "Get out of this country! Get out before the Yukon freezes tight as a rope!"

"We don't want to get out," the older Murray said as the boy listened tensely.

"The good creeks are gone," Larry Arp said. "Dominion, Sulphur, Quartz—there's nothin' much to stake. If I was in your boots, I'd go to Bear Creek or the Hunker, and stake a hillside claim."

"You have to dig deep on those hillside claims," Mike Murray said. "I've heard about them. It'd be awful hard work for a boy."

"No, it wouldn't, Pop!" Joe hastened to say.

His father smiled at him. "Even with your sister to help you, it'd be awful hard work."

It was the miner Larry Arp who showed Joe how to bake the famous sour-dough bread that had become a nickname for the old-timers. "You put the sour dough in a gold pan," Larry Arp said. "Cover it with another pan."

Then Larry Arp built a fire and heated a heap of gravel. He shoveled the hot gravel on top of the pan and said, "That'll make a round loaf, sixteen by eight. Remember, boy, if you stay this winter, keep away from *cheechako* baking powder. That'll give you scurvy, sure as fate!"

The two Murrays hit the trail back to Dawson City the very next day. Late in the afternoon they reached the forks of the Eldorado and Bonanza Creeks, where a two-story hotel was located.

They went into the hotel and Mike Murray told the woman who walked toward them that all they wanted was to sit in the shade awhile.

"No charge for shade," she smiled.

Joe wiped his sweaty face and glanced at a table where six or seven sourdoughs were eating pickled moose nose—an Arctic delicacy. His mouth watered when a waiter brought over to the men a platter of broiled moose steaks. The boy was tired of beans and bacon.

The miners pulled out fat little sacks of gold dust to pay for their meal. The woman weighed the dust on her gold scales.

"It's only us *cheechakos* who use paper money," Mike Murray remarked to Joe. "I wonder if we'll ever have any gold dust?"

"Sure, we will, Pop," Joe said.

"Maybe, son," his father answered, shrugging. "Maybe."

A miner with a battered old hat on his head walked over to them. "Hard times, pardner?" he asked, smiling. "I can see you're just a couple of *cheechakos*. Not even a pair. Just one and a half."

He was so friendly, Mike Murray poured out all their disappointment. "We came too late," Mike concluded.

"How about a bit of chocolate?" the miner, whose name was Bailey, asked Joe. "I like a boy with grit."

He led them to his room. It was furnished with a cot, a chair, a table, and a wash basin. Bailey pulled a leather bag from under the cot. He opened it and gave Joe a square of dark brown chocolate. The boy thanked the miner, and offered his father half of it.

"Chocolate's for the young ones," Mike Murray said to Bailey with a smile.

Joe popped the chocolate into his mouth. He didn't chew it but let it melt slowly.

"It's all luck on the creeks," Bailey said to Mike Murray. "Some of the men you see ain't makin' wages."

"Wages?" Joe's father asked, puzzled.

"By wages, we mean washin' out an ounce of gold a day—sixteen dollars," Bailey explained. "A man can't work for less. It don't pay. Food, supplies, it all costs money. And right next to the man sweatin' for wages the next man's washin' out a thousand a day. Take me. My claim on the Bonanza paid me one hundred and eighty thousand dollars! I've sold out. Next week I'll be on the steamer to St. Michael. One Klondike winter is enough for a man unless he's an Eskimo."

"I guess you sold your claim for plenty," Mike Murray said.

"I didn't have a full claim. All I owned was a hundred feet. I sold seventy feet and I've got thirty left."

"You aim to sell the thirty?" Joe's father asked, trying to conceal his eagerness.

Bailey laughed. "You ain't got the money to buy thirty feet on the Bonanza."

Joe gulped as he glanced at his father. "Maybe I have," his father said slowly.

"For a man with money it's a good investment,"

Bailey said. "The muck's been cleared off it. There's a new prospect hole started. Dig another ten or fifteen feet and you're on the paystreak—"

"How much do you want?" Mike Murray interrupted.

"Six thousand dollars."

"I haven't got that much." He lifted his long body from the chair. "Well, thanks for the chocolate."

"Hold on!" the sourdough said. "I feel kind of sorry for you *cheechakos*. I got plenty of money. How much you got in your poke?"

"Less than four thousand and I need some of that for tools," Mike Murray said, his voice trembling.

"I'll do you a favor," Bailey smiled. "I'll sell you twenty feet of my thirty for three thousand dollars. And I'll throw in some tools I got in a shack."

The sourdough walked over to Joe and slid his fingers through the boy's thick blond hair. "I like the grit of this youngster," he said. "We can go look at my claim right now. If you don't see gold in the pan you don't have to buy."

Joe's eyes were suddenly as bright as his father's. The room, so bare and plain, seemed to glitter. And Bailey himself, whiskered and black-nailed, seemed to be all aglitter, too. It was as if some magic had changed the room into gold and the man into a Santa Claus of the Klondike.

CHAPTER SIX

Panic

"SEEING is believing," Bailey said when they arrived at the thirty feet he still owned. He walked over to the prospect hole on the twenty-foot strip he proposed to sell. "You go down, Mike, and fill up the bucket."

Mike Murray climbed down into the hole. Joe, staring over the edge, watched his father shovel gravel into the bucket.

Bailey spat on his hands and turned the handle of the windlass. "Dig and dump," he grinned at Joe. "That's the life of a miner."

When Joe's father came up from the hole Bailey filled a pan with the newly dug gravel. Then he added water to it down at the creek. He washed the pan out. At the sight of the yellow specks of gold, Joe became so excited, he wanted to run, to shout, to tell all the miners on Bonanza Creek that now his father owned a gold mine, too!

Mike Murray and Bailey returned to Dawson City to record the sale of the twenty-foot strip at the Mine Recorder's Office. They left Joe behind. "Time's money," Bailey had said to the boy. "You chop that hole deeper while the ground's soft. Winter'll be here soon enough!"

That night, inside Bailey's shack on the twenty-foot strip, Joe wrote a letter to his sister Anne.

In the Klondike,
September 22nd, 1897.

Dear Sister,

At last we have a gold mine. We own 20 feet on Bonanza Creek. The prospect hole looks good. It is 14 feet down. Mr. Bailey says that in another 15 or 20 feet we will hit the paystreak. Mr. Bailey sold it to us. He is a nice man.

Pop is very happy and so am I. I will write more news in this same letter when Pop gets back from Dawson City . . .

Joe put the letter aside. Blowing out the candle, he stretched out on a pile of spruce boughs, all the bed there was in the shack. He thought that Annie might be puzzled by his letter. He should have explained that a prospect hole was always sunk blind. There were no surface clues. If the test pans going down showed gold, the miner knew he was on the track of the paystreak. There was so much to explain! The strip they had bought was pitted with prospect holes that had proved worthless. It was all luck, Joe thought sleepily. He should have told Annie about luck . . .

He awoke early and fried himself a mess of beans in bacon fat. As he was eating, a man appeared at the door of the shack. He was a gaunt miner with a dirty yellowish beard, one of the four miners who had bought seventy feet of Bailey's original hundred. Bailey had pointed them out yesterday.

"Expect your father today?" the miner asked Joe.

"Yes," Joe nodded. "Pop said he'd hire pack horses to bring our outfit out."

The visitor sat down on a stool. "Know what we call the strip your father bought?" he asked.

"No," Joe said.

"We call it the hard-luck strip," the miner said. "Five holes been sunk on it and nothin' worth a nickel."

"Maybe the sixth one's the lucky one," Joe said hopefully.

"Lucky for who?" the miner demanded almost angrily. "Ever hear of salting a mine? O' course not! Know what they do? They mix some gold dust in with a charge of gunpowder and shoot it into the gravel."

Joe winced. The beans he was chewing suddenly tasted like pine cones.

"Mind you, me and my partners ain't sure Bailey salted that hole to fool a *cheechako* buyer. Maybe he did and maybe he didn't."

The visitor stood up and jabbed a long, dirty finger at a strip of bacon in Joe's frying pan. "This Bonanza's a creek like that piece o' bacon," he said. "Made up o' fat and lean. This hard luck

strip is just plain lean and you might as well know it."

"How can I tell Pop?" Joe said, choking. "Poor Pop—"

"You're his partner, ain't you?" the miner said.

"I'll get Bailey arrested!" the boy cried.

"Hold your hosses, bub," the miner said. "Me and my partners ain't sure Bailey salted that hole. All we're sure of is he sold you a mighty lean strip. There's no law against that! All you can do is hit the trail to Dawson and try and get Bailey to give you some of your money back."

"Why did he do it?" Joe was on the verge of tears. "He'd made his fortune."

"Some are never satisfied," the miner answered. "If the Mounties weren't here there'd be murder up and down these creeks."

Joe would never forget that nightmare day. He half-ran and half-walked the ten miles to Dawson City. But he had come too late. His father had already paid Bailey three thousand dollars for the twenty-foot strip. And Bailey hotly denied salting it. Neither would he return their money. In desperation, the two Murrays went to police headquarters. A Mountie sergeant listened to their story and said, "You have no proof the hole was salted. We cannot force Bailey to return your money."

That night they slept on the *Annie,* or rather they tried to sleep. The buzzing mosquitoes crawled all over their netting. And just as insistent were the stinging thoughts in the minds of father and son. Three thousand dollars thrown away on a salted claim! Hardly any money left! No tools, no hopes!

Morning came at last. The boy had never seen his father look so bad. The strong, dark face had aged overnight.

"Summer's about gone," Mike Murray muttered. "If we're leaving, it has to be soon."

"Wait, Pop," the boy pleaded.

"Wait? That's how I feel, too. Wait and hope for something. But what are we waiting for? Another salted mine?"

Day after day of indecision drifted by for the two Murrays. On Front Street, there were rumors of new gold strikes in the Indian River country. But Mike Murray didn't have the spirit to go prospecting. All he seemed able to do was join the crowds of *cheechakos* who spent all their time swapping hard-luck stories. The boy tagged after his father like a shadow. Often, with a pang, he remembered his mother's farewell words to take care of each other.

In the meantime, the Yukon was falling rapidly. Day by day, there was less water in the river. The ships that had been expected to relieve the food shortage were stuck on sandbars. When the news reached Dawson City there was panic. The news traveled out to the creeks, and hundreds of miners flocked into Dawson City. Without the grub they had ordered, they wouldn't be able to stay the winter.

"The *Bella* 'll get through!" they predicted hopefully. "If she doesn't, the *Alice* will or the *John J. Healey*. Or the *Portius B. Weare*."

On September 28th, the *Portius B. Weare* came into Dawson City with a story that stunned the waiting crowd. The ship had been boarded at Circle City by armed miners who had paid Dawson City prices for the food they had taken off, to see them through the winter. When the *Bella* puffed in two days later, her captain told a similar story. Both ships brought in some food but not enough for all the miners in Dawson City.

Beans, the miners' staple, that were eaten with almost every meal, jumped in price to a dollar a pound. The Canadian authorities urged the population to go downriver to Fort Yukon where there were ample food supplies. Soon the river would be frozen and it would be too late to go!

The miners held meetings and demanded that the gamblers be sent back to St. Michael, the Alaskan port on salt water. "No food for the gamblers and the sports!" the miners shouted.

And then one morning the Inspector of Mounted Police issued a proclamation urging everyone to leave before the food supply gave out entirely.

Yet Joe and his father remained in Dawson City. In the give-and-take of the miners' meetings they had become friendly with an old sourdough whose name was Caribou Dave Dresser. It was a friendship based on mutual need. The Murrays had precious food in a warehouse on Front Street while Caribou Dave had secret knowledge of a possible new gold stampede.

"I've got this good friend, Sid Edwards," he had confided to Mike Murray and Joe. "He's prospectin' the smaller tributaries or pups, as we call 'em, of the Indian River. Most of the Indian's pups've been staked—Gold Run and Nine Mile and the Eureka and the rest. But there's some left and one of these days Sid Edwards'll be showin' up. He promised to let me know if he made a discovery."

Caribou Dave had been in the country a year ago when nearly every old-timer had struck it rich. But a broken leg and pneumonia had stranded him in Fort Yukon all winter and spring. "I got the hard luck of Job in the Bible," he had said.

"We're as hard luck as you," Joe's father had replied grimly.

"Not with all the grub you got," Caribou Dave had smiled. "Anyway, it's our last chance. A hard-luck sourdough like me. A hard-luck *cheechako* like you with a boy thrown into the lot. We'll make three good partners."

Early one morning Caribou Dave hobbled down to the *Annie* where Mike Murray and his son were still sleeping. He woke them up. They stared at him without a word. There was no need to ask any questions. The sourdough's whiskered face was tense, his gray-blue eyes burning with the gold fever.

"Sid is in town," Caribou Dave whispered as if he were afraid that the men sleeping in the other boats might hear him. "He's made a brand-new discovery on a creek he calls Gold Creek! He'll record it soon as the office opens!"

Silently, Mike Murray picked up a length of iron rod on the bottom of the *Annie*. He pried open the top of a box and took out what had been kept in readiness for just this news. A blanket, a knapsack holding two weeks' grub, and four claim posts.

Each post was four inches square and three feet long. Canadian Mining Law stated that the claim posts had to be driven eighteen inches into the ground, with eighteen inches showing above ground.

"Joe, wrap those posts up in the blanket," Caribou Dave ordered. "If people see 'em there'll be a stampede. Mike, you know what you have to do. Drive them posts into the four corners of the claim. You're entitled to five hundred feet. Blast it!" he groaned. "I wisht I didn't have this game leg!" He slapped viciously at the leg he had broken.

Joe unfolded the blanket and stowed away the four claim posts. "Pop," he whispered. "Can't I go with you?"

"Don't be a pest!" Caribou Dave snapped. "We've told you why a hundred times. Mike'll have to be on the trail day and night. Have to run his heart out! Think this news about Gold Creek is just ours? Sure, Sid Edwards made the discovery claim, but there were three, four other prospectors out there and they're all here in Dawson right now! All got friends. It'll be a stampede! Stop gawkin', boy, and get your father some breakfast!"

As Mike Murray bolted down some food, Caribou Dave strapped the knapsack and blanket onto his back.

"It's the last chance for all of us," the old sourdough whispered.

"Gold Creek or bust!" Joe's father said fiercely. He grabbed Joe and hugged him, a fierce bearhug. Then he jumped from the *Annie* to the shore.

"Pop, take care of yourself," the boy called.

CHAPTER SEVEN

Camp on Gold Creek

MIKE MURRAY had succeeded in staking the sixth claim above the discovery claim of Sid Edwards. "Six-Above," Caribou Dave called it in miners' lingo.

They had packed their grub and supplies out to Gold Creek. The day after their arrival they were on the wooded slopes with their axes. "Cabin comes first," Caribou Dave said. "We want it eight feet wide, twelve feet long and eight logs high."

The three partners of Six-Above worked as long as the light held. Already, now that October was here, the daylight had begun to fade. At last the cabin was finished. They chinked the spaces between the logs with moss and mud. The floor was made of boards from the *Annie* which they had knocked to pieces and packed out with their outfit. Enough boards were left over for three wall bunks and a table.

"The *Annie* sure came in useful," the father of the real Annie said, stomping his boot on the new floor.

"Pop, we ought to call our cabin the 'Annie,' " Joe suggested.

"Call it the 'Hotel Annie'!" Caribou Dave grinned. "This here Klondike hotel is as good as that Hotel Waldorf in New York!"

The chairs in the Hotel Annie consisted of empty packing boxes. When they set the Yukon stove into the cabin, the pipe leading up through an oil drum on the roof, Caribou Dave's eyes began to twinkle. "Now I'm beginnin' to feel warm," he said.

Caribou Dave Dresser had been in Alaska since 1894. He had lived with the Indians and learned the Indian ways. "You take charge," Mike Murray had told him the very first day on Gold Creek. "Joe and me are only *cheechakos.*"

"Can't have an army with all generals," the old sourdough had agreed. But when he wanted anything done he nearly always asked for it with a joke on his lips.

"We want to be millionaires," he liked to say. "But first we better be sure we don't freeze to death. Joe, you can start choppin' firewood."

On the sloping ledges, the timber was stunted because of the seven-month winters. But it was plentiful. All day long, up and down the new mining camp, the sound of axes rang. Joe felled spruce and sawed firelogs until his arms ached.

That was his job while his father and Caribou Dave cleared the muck and started a prospect hole. The ground was still soft but each night the frosts thickened, and one morning the first snow fell.

"Joe," Caribou Dave said as they sat inside their snug cabin, the wood blazing in the stove. "Don't think it's cold yet. It only gets cold when the creeks freeze to the banks—and that's not cold. It only gets cold when the floatin' ice on the Yukon piles up on the bars and islands—and that's not cold. It only gets cold when the Yukon's tight to the shore and the daylight's gone—and that's not cold. Only gets cold when a man has to shave his beard so his breath won't turn into ice in his whiskers!"

Mornings, they left their cabin for a dazzling white world. The snows had covered the ruts in the trail to faraway Dawson City. Joe was glad he was wearing two pair of woolen socks inside his boots. His parka of drill cloth reached below his knees and the hood was lined with fur. Over the woolen mittens on his hands, he wore the caribou mittens Diamond Jack had given him in Dyea.

On a homemade sled he hauled firewood to the prospect hole. The ground was hard as rock, and now they had to burn their way down to the pay dirt.

"Work easy," Caribou Dave said to Joe. "Never get up a sweat. You sweat and it'll turn to ice and you'll freeze to death inside all your furs."

Joe narrowed his eyes against the white glare. He shielded his eyes with his mittened hand. Caribou Dave noticed the gesture.

"Joe, never come out again without your black glasses," he warned the boy.

They built a bonfire in the prospect hole and Mike Murray said, "I hope we hit bedrock soon."

"Might have to burn our way down twenty, thirty feet," Caribou Dave said as the flames licked up out of the hole.

Fires burned day and night in all the prospect holes started by the Gold Creek miners. When Joe stepped outside the cabin to bring in a bucket of icicles—"Yukon drinking water," to be melted inside, he would sniff at the smoky haze that covered the valley. Live flame shot up out of the pits, lighting the snow.

The fires burned ten hours at a time and then the ashes would be removed and the thawed gravel shoveled out and tested to see if it contained gold.

"You test this pan, Joe," Caribou Dave said to the boy one day.

Inside the warm cabin, the sourdough filled the pan of freshly dug gravel with water. Joe's eyes popped as he began to wash out the pan over the watertight panning box. "Easy, easy," the sourdough corrected his technique. "Gold's heavy. It'll go to the bottom."

Joe stared down at the scattered yellow specks in the pan. "We've struck it rich!" he exclaimed excitedly.

Caribou Dave laughed. "That pan ain't worth five dollars. Remember, Joe, there's three of us partners on Six-Above. We have to pan three ounces a day to make it worth while. Something around forty-five, fifty dollars."

It was burn and dig and test every foot of the way. It was a hard life. But sometimes on winter nights when they weren't too tired they would visit their neighbors. They sat one evening in the cabin of Dratfeld and Mogantte, the two miners on the claim below their own—the Five-Above.

"We're down twenty-six feet and we've found nothing," Dratfeld said. "We're starting another hole tomorrow." He was a grocer from Des Moines, Iowa, turned gold miner. His partner, Mogantte, was a French sailor who had run away from his ship at San Francisco to go north.

Caribou Dave picked up a candle from the table and held it close to Dratfeld's face, beardless now. With the sub-zero weather all the men had been forced to shave. "You better do a little eatin'!" Caribou Dave said.

"We're eating," Dratfeld said in surprise.

"Eatin' what?" Caribou Dave snorted. "Beans and more beans and still more beans! And flap-jacks made of bakin' powder no better than marble dust! And *cheechako* coffee instead of good Hudson Bay tea!"

Dratfeld smiled wearily. "I went into Dawson last week. There isn't a can of anything to be had. Beans, they got! Flour, they got! But that's all!"

The French sailor, Mogantte, shrugged. "We eat when we rich. Beeg gold on Eldorado!" he said, his dark eyes shining in the candlelight.

"I told Frenchy what I heard in Dawson City," Dratfeld explained. "They'll make a fortune on that creek when they clean up in the summer."

Mike Murray picked up a log and tossed it into the stove. "Do you men know it's almost Thanksgiving?"

Joe glanced at his father. He thought of how last Thanksgiving the whole family had been together, his mother and sister and uncle. He felt homesick and a little sad. He thought of his sister Anne and wondered what she would have said if she could have seen them now.

"I'm glad somebody mentioned Thanksgiving," Caribou Dave said. "We're havin' roast turkey and you're all invited! We're roastin' Mike's old boot. For lettuce we'll pick some Arctic moss. For white potatoes we'll cut the centers out of some icicles."

When Thanksgiving came, the three partners celebrated. But their turkey was bacon. And with the beans they opened up one of their last cans of tomatoes. Their pumpkin pie was a doughnut a foot wide and studded with lumps of sugar. As a preventive against scurvy they drank tea made from spruce needles. And for entertainment Mike read from the Bible he had brought with him.

And always the work went on. The hills of waste dirt rose higher. "A man can dig all year and find nothin'," Caribou Dave told Mike, "while ten feet away on the next claim they'll be pickin' up nuggets. I think we better start a second hole, Mike."

The daylight was almost gone now. The miners

of Gold Creek worked in a ghostly twilight in which the only sound was the squeaking of the wooden windlass cranks. Underground they tunneled out of their prospect holes like moles, looking for the pay dirt. The candles they stuck in the dirt walls cast a thin, steady light. There were accidents. Rocks dropped down on the men in the holes and tunnels.

One day, when the digging was done, Joe climbed down in the new prospect hole to light the all-night fire. This second hole had been burned down eighteen feet, so deep there was no draft. Joe waited. He had to be sure the fire would stay lit.

He waited too long. Black smoke thrashed all around him like a great big wing. He choked and dashed for the ladder. The smoke thickened. He climbed and felt himself becoming dizzy. The bones in his fingers seemed to melt.

"Joe!" he heard a dim, faraway voice calling.

He couldn't answer, clinging to the ladder. The next thing he knew, a hand had grabbed the hood of his parka and the dim voice was saying, "Joe, get moving!"

It was a reeling boy who staggered out of the prospect hole. His father washed his face with snow and carried him into the cabin.

In all the cabins, there were men who had been hurt in rock falls or who had suffered frostbite.

"Bad luck comes in streaks," Caribou Dave said when, just before Christmas, Mike Murray complained of pains in his legs.

That was a sign of scurvy. The old sourdough examined Mike's gums and teeth. The gums had begun to swell—another sign of scurvy!

"Sour-dough bread and spruce needle tea ain't enough for you," Caribou Dave said as Joe listened anxiously. "The man needs fresh stuff. Blast it! Even if we had a poke full of gold dust, we couldn't buy a thing in Dawson. There's only one thing to do. Go for a moose or a caribou."

"We haven't got a dog sled," Mike Murray said.

"I could borrow one if I share what I get," Caribou Dave replied. "Yes, sir, Mike! I'll see if me and Joe can kill us some fresh meat."

CHAPTER EIGHT

The Hunt

MUSH!" Caribou Dave shouted at the borrowed team of six Malamutes hitched to the sled. The dogs pulled, and the man trotted forward on his snowshoes.

Riding on the sled, wrapped in fur robes, Joe smiled with joy at the easy movement of the sled on the white packed snow.

"Bring back a moose steak!" his father shouted from the door of their cabin.

The sled glided across the snow like a drop of water sliding down a cup. Joe turned and waved good-by at his father, who became smaller and smaller. The cabin, too, shrank. It became a toy cabin, but still his father's distant voice reached him.

"Bring back a moose steak!"

The boy remembered his uncle's farewell when

The sled glided across the snow

they had sailed from Seattle: "Bring back the gold!"

If his folks could see them now, the boy brooded. He peered through his dark glasses at the dogs mushing up the slope. The stumps of the trees hacked down by the Gold Creek miners loomed like gravestones in the twilight that was all that the sun could muster these days.

In a few minutes they were in the wilderness. Through Joe's dark glasses, the stunted spruce were black as ink, the snow grayish. He stared intently at the tails of the six sled dogs.

"Malamute tails are the best thermometer there is," Caribou Dave had said. "When the curl goes out of 'em it's cold."

The tails of the six dogs curled jauntily as they ran. They crossed a frozen bog. They skirted desolate barrens, and the only sound was the clanking of the dog chain that Caribou Dave held in one gloved hand. Now and then the sourdough would call out, "Haw!" and the dogs would veer off to the left. Or he would call, "Gee!" and they would travel to the right.

After about two hours, Caribou Dave shouted, "Whoa!" The dogs stopped and the man said,

"Joe, I'll ride now. I'm beginnin' to feel a little warm."

Joe knew that was the danger sign. A man didn't dare sweat in the icy wilderness. The sweat would freeze and a man could die inside his warm parka.

Joe put on a pair of snowshoes and said, "Can I take the chain, Caribou?"

The sourdough only grinned. "Those wolves won't listen to you, Joe."

"I'd like to try, Caribou."

"Go ahead and try!"

Joe shook the dog chain and shouted, "Mush!"

The lead dog turned around and looked at the boy. None of the dogs moved. "Mush! Mush!" Joe called. The dogs imitated stones.

Caribou Dave laughed and took the dog chain. "Mush!" he shouted. Instantly, the six dogs muscled forward, tugging against their harness. "Those Malamutes understand me 'cause I'm half Malamute myself," Caribou Dave said to the boy trotting alongside the sled.

Once the dogs stopped without a command. Joe glanced excitedly at Caribou Dave, his lips shaping the word he didn't dare speak. *Moose!*

"No," the sourdough said. "They don't smell moose. That third varmint's cut his foot and wants his bedroom slipper."

The third dog was holding up one of his front paws like a human being. Caribou Dave opened a sack and pulled out a moosehide dog-moccasin.

"I'll put it on," Joe offered.

"He might snap at you," Caribou Dave said as he went to the injured dog. He tied on the moccasin. "They're half wolf and half lawyer," he joked. "I've told you about the two Malamutes in Dawson City who liked fruit. You could see the pair of them on Front Street every day. One'd be carryin' a fruit jar and t'other a knife."

"A knife?" Joe asked, smiling with anticipation.

"Sure, to pry open the lid of the jar," Caribou Dave said with a straight face. "Let's eat, long as we've stopped."

He took kindling and firewood from another sack on the sled and made a small fire. He boiled tea and heated beans. When they had finished eating, Caribou Dave said to Joe, "The curl's goin' out of their tails."

He walked to the sled and examined the thermometer every dog sled in the North always carried. "Thirty below," he announced. "Ten more degrees before the mercury freezes. Joe, about those two fruit-lovin' Malamutes? Sometimes the one with the knife'd be totin' a rock. Break the jar with the rock. But they didn't like that. Too much glass got into the fruit."

Late in the day they came to a hunter's shack they had been told about in Gold Creek. "We'll sleep here tonight, Joe," the sourdough said.

The man and the boy unloaded the sled. Then, snowshoes on their feet and rifles in their hands, they ranged out from the shack. "The moose've gone into the deep snow to get away from the wolves," Caribou Dave whispered.

The twilight was deepening by the second. All was still and hushed. Far in the distance they saw dark specks on the white barren. "Might be caribou," the sourdough said. "Caribou are curious as turkeys. Let's creep up on them while we still got light."

The caribou smelled the hunters while still out of rifle-shot. The barren emptied of life. "Blast it!" Caribou Dave exclaimed. "We won't eat meat tonight."

The next day, after breakfasting in the shack, they started a huge bull moose out of the gloom of a patch of spruces.

Joe's heart seemed to split in two. The moose had appeared like an apparition, black and shaggy, and running like a deer. Joe raised his rifle and heard Caribou Dave's rifle go off. The moose bolted out toward the barren, untouched.

"You couldn't have hit him," Joe said consolingly, as he lowered his weapon.

"Why didn't *you* shoot?" the man demanded.

"I never had him in my sights, Caribou."

"You should've fired anyway!" the sourdough said in a voice that sounded like a stranger's to Joe. "This is the Klondike. If you don't allow for luck you might as well curl up and die!"

Silently, they returned to the shack and the dogs. Caribou Dave drove the team over to the moose's tracks. The dogs snuffed eagerly. "Get on the sled!" Caribou Dave said to the boy.

The sled flew forward. Joe stared unhappily at

the snowy wasteland, gray in the thin light. He couldn't forget the accusing tone in Caribou Dave's voice. He thought of his sick father and his sense of shame deepened.

The wind had died down. The air felt like fire when Joe breathed it into his lungs. He forced himself to breathe more and more slowly, but still that frigid air burned his nostrils and throat and lungs. He peered through his dark snow-glasses at the tails of the dogs. The curl had gone out of them. It must be forty below, maybe colder, he thought.

Joe glanced up at Caribou Dave mushing alongside the sled, relentlessly driving the team and himself after the bull moose. The boy hesitated for only another second. "Look at the thermometer!" he cried. "Look at the thermometer!"

"Gettin' a little too cold for you, *cheechako?*" Caribou Dave sneered, halting the team.

"I'm not thinking of me. I'm thinking of the dogs! You told me yourself you can't make dogs work at forty below."

"The dogs," Caribou Dave muttered.

"It'll kill them," Joe persisted. "You said this team's worth two thousand dollars."

Caribou Dave didn't seem to hear him. His gray-blue eyes under his parka were distant.

"You'll kill those dogs!" the boy said.

Slowly, as if coming out of a trance, Caribou Dave glanced at the sled thermometer. He tried to shake it, but it wouldn't shake. The mercury was frozen. He walked slowly over to the team and unharnessed the animals. The six Malamutes burrowed down into the snow for protection. "Get under the robes!" Caribou Dave ordered the boy.

He crawled under, also. It was the only shelter between them and the killing cold. Huddled together, they stayed there three hours. The thermometer was still frozen. "We've got to take a chance and get back to the shack," Caribou Dave said.

Neither of them rode on the sled, afraid to tire the dogs. They crossed a bog and Joe heard the gnawing sound in the ice underneath his snowshoes. The ice worms! he thought, remembering how the sourdoughs described the sound. He breathed as slowly as he could, but the air stabbed like a knife.

That night they slept in the shack with all six Malamutes for companions.

In the morning, as they ate their breakfast, Caribou Dave said, "I was mean yesterday, Joe. You were right." He shook his head and said, "This Klondike is makin' us all turn mean as wolves."

Joe smiled. "I'm glad you're not mad at me any more, Caribou."

"Wolves!" Caribou Dave exclaimed. "We're goin' to let the wolves do our huntin' for us!"

"You're joking," the boy said.

"Not this time, Joe. When it's cold like this the wolves go huntin' for a moose in a big pack. They try to drive a moose out onto a creek, hopin' the moose'll slip on the ice. The hunter whose shack this is told me of a spot they've used."

"Honest?" Joe asked.

"Honest. Let's take a look at the thermometer."

It had risen. It was thirty-two degrees below zero.

Three hours later, they reached the spot, a shallow valley with a frozen creek on the bottom. They mushed up the creek until they saw the skeleton of a moose. Caribou Dave looked down on the gleaming polished bones. "Wolves," he murmured. "They didn't leave a scrap of meat neither."

"How do you know they'll be driving another moose this way?" Joe asked.

"I don't know," Caribou Dave said, "but it's worth a try, Joe."

He drove the team up the slope of the valley into the woods. "It's sit and wait," Caribou Dave said. "I learned to do that when I lived with the Siwash Indians."

The hours dragged by slowly. Joe had forgotten and left his glasses in the shack. He began to squint and frown, but he wouldn't take Caribou Dave's pair. They ate cold beans and waited. The ghostly light faded and the night was brighter than the day had been. The stars glittered, and the bluish-white snow shone like glass.

They slept on the sled, under the blankets and fur robes. They awoke with the first wan light and Caribou Dave said, "We'll try somethin' else. We'll go up the creek and maybe we'll see 'em."

Joe was glad to be on the move again. When it was his turn to ride on the sled, he kept his eyes shut. When he trotted alongside, he wore Caribou Dave's glasses.

One long white hour followed another, but there was no sight or sound of wolves. And then in the late afternoon, far away, so far away that he thought he was dreaming, Joe saw a large dark speck followed by six or seven much smaller specks. He rubbed his eyes and stared.

Caribou Dave grabbed the boy's shoulder and pointed.

In a second they were in wild pursuit. The dogs had never mushed so fast. Caribou Dave's hoarse voice was like a whip. The specks grew larger, swinging down the long, low slope.

Joe's heart was thumping as furiously as if he were sprinting alongside of Caribou Dave and not riding on the sled. Now and then one of the dogs snarled as they tore along.

But none of the specks swerved. Not the moose running for its life. Not the six or seven wolves beyond fear of dogs and men. Starvation had overcome their caution.

The largest of the specks was now recognizably a moose. Joe, staring ahead as if his life depended upon it, watched the six or seven smaller specks change into wolves.

Down the slope they all came, the four-footed hunters and the hunted. Larger and larger and larger!

The air rang with the cries of the six Malamutes, and suddenly the wolves stopped and faced their dog and human enemies.

A rifle shot spat out and one of the wolves darted up from the snow and fell motionless. Instantly, the others in the pack sprang on it as if all the time they had planned to do just this thing.

"The moose!" Joe heard Caribou Dave shout-

Down the slope they came,
the hunters and the hunted

ing behind him. And only now did he realize that Caribou had dropped the dog chain to fire at the wolves. "Joe, get as close as you can and shoot!"

The boy's head whirled around and he saw the sourdough in shooting position again. But this bullet was aimed at the flying moose.

God, the boy prayed, let him hit it.

Joe didn't have the dog chain in his hand, but there was no need to urge the team on. The boy knew that Caribou had missed the moose, for the animal was still running strong. Joe trembled, and fumbled for his rifle as the sled came closer and closer to the moose.

The moose reached the creek and slipped on the ice. The boy flung himself from the sled. He felt as if a mountain had fallen on him. He forced himself to sit up in the snow and, biting on his lips to steady himself, he raised the rifle to his shoulder.

For one heart-breaking second he held the black target in sight, and holding it, he pressed the trigger gently.

Two rifle shots burst the air. The moose slumped into a heap, dead. The dogs hurled themselves, harness, sled, and all, upon the moose.

"Stop 'em!"

This was Caribou Dave shouting over at Joe. The sourdough, after firing at the moose, had come running as fast as he could. The boy jumped to his feet and, rifle in hand, he also sprinted toward the ravening Malamutes.

He reached them before the sourdough. He put the safety on his rifle and, using the weapon as a club, ran at the blood-crazed dogs. They snarled at him, but steadily he attacked them.

"Whoa! Whoa!" Caribou Dave shouted, jumping into the dogs and driving them from the moose.

The man and the boy forced the dogs to retreat.

Caribou Dave stooped and with his long knife opened up the moose. He tossed the entrails to the team, and only now a smile touched his lips. "Meat!" he cried, almost as fierce as one of the dogs.

The boy was shaking with excitement.

"Joe!" Caribou Dave said. "You're not hurt?"

"No."

The man stared at him and then sighed.

"Thank God," he said. "Joe, anybody who calls you a *cheechako* is a fool. Joe, you're as good as any sourdough who ever lived."

Up on the slope of the valley, the pack that had devoured the wolf shot by Caribou Dave stared down at the two powerful enemies who had robbed them of the moose.

"We'll get this moose cut up," Caribou Dave said to the boy, "and head for home. Or how would you like a steak now, you old sourdough?"

CHAPTER NINE

Birthday in the Klondike

JOE was snow-blind when they returned to their cabin on Gold Creek. Caribou Dave brewed tea and placed the steeped tea leaves on the boy's eyelids. The old sourdough was as gentle as gentle could be. The snow-blindness didn't worry him. The boy's feverish forehead did. Pneumonia! That was what worried Caribou Dave.

"When will Joe be able to see?" his father asked anxiously.

"Couple of days at most," Caribou Dave said.

Joe, listening to their voices, felt as if he were inside a black cave. So this is how it feels to be blind, he thought. An endless blackness . . .

"Nothin' fresh meat won't cure," he heard Caribou Dave saying to his father. "Once he gets some of this moose into him he'll be as good as new. And so will you, Mike."

Joe could see the next morning, although his eyes throbbed and it hurt to look at the kerosene lamp. By suppertime, his eyes were almost normal. He was a happy boy when they sat down at the table. His head felt giddy and he had a dry little cough, but the sight of that table was almost a cure in itself.

A big tin plate was piled high with juicy moose steaks. There was a plate of dried fruit and a can of tomatoes that Caribou Dave had acquired in a swap for some of the moose meat. The pitcher of melted snow water was flavored with citric acid, also obtained by swapping. The citric acid, like lemons, was good for scurvy.

"Mike, your scurvy is good as licked," Caribou Dave declared.

Before the week was up Mike was strong enough to work. But Joe had a touch of bronchitis. Or, so Caribou Dave thought it. Feverish and sick, the boy lay in his bunk. He tried reading his father's Bible to pass the time, but the words wouldn't stand still.

"It's my fault!" Caribou Dave blamed himself. "The thermometer froze and like a fool I kept on mushin'. I'm the biggest fool in the Klondike!"

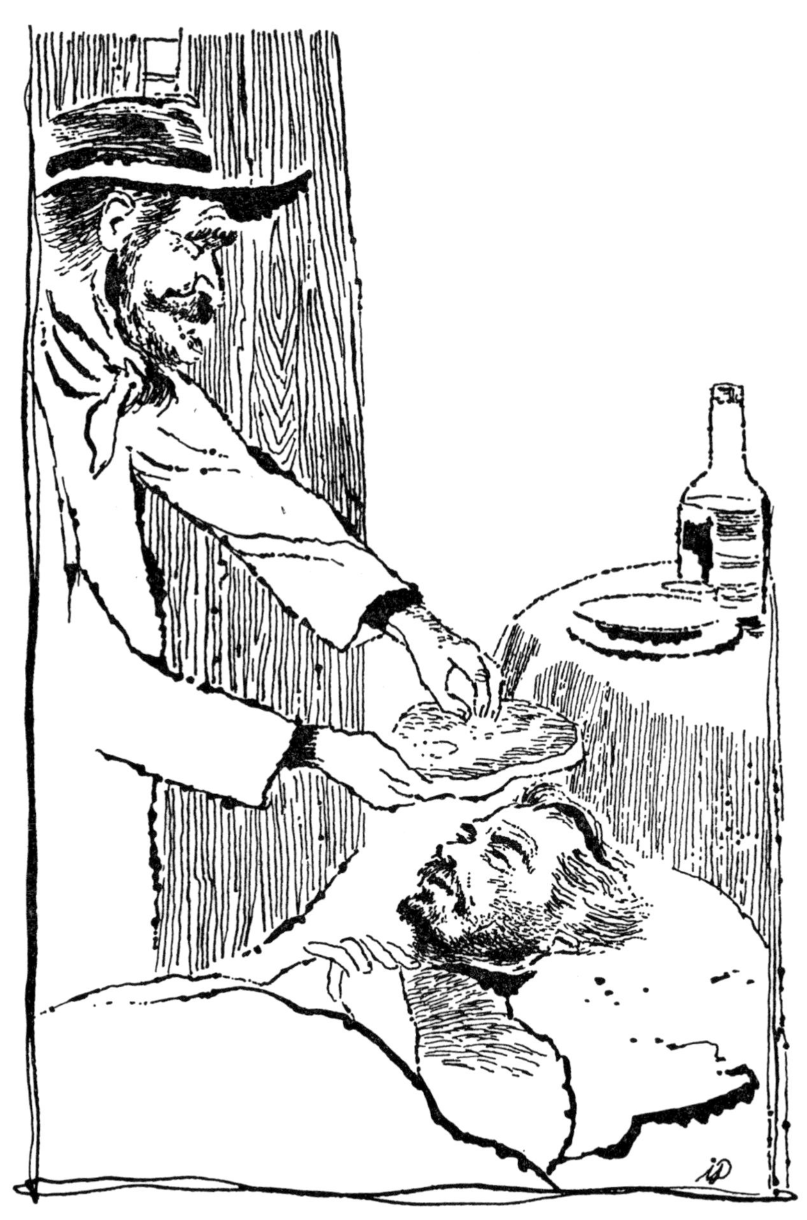

"Mike, your scurvy is as good as licked,"
Caribou Dave declared

The conscience-stricken sourdough waited on Joe like a hospital nurse. Every night after work he sat by Joe's bunk and told him stories.

"Joe, I haven't told you about the miner who came in from the diggings when it was fifty below. Just a fool like me. A pack of wolves came for him and he run for the trees. He got up all right, but all his clothes were torn off. That hungry bunch circled that tree all night. There he was shiverin' and naked, but he didn't freeze to death. You know why, Joe? The breath of the wolves kept him warm."

Joe tried to smile, but his head was spinning.

"I got the poor boy sick," Caribou Dave said to Mike Murray.

"He'll get better," Mike replied in a cheerful voice. But when Joe was asleep, his father's face became solemn. "Caribou," he said, "maybe we ought to take him to Dawson City to see a doctor."

"That boy can't travel, Mike."

"His birthday's soon," Mike sighed. "January eighteenth. He'll be fifteen. His first birthday away from home."

"I know just what he'll want!" Caribou said.

On Joe's birthday, late in the day, Caribou Dave

dragged a six-month-old Malamute puppy into the cabin. "That dog's yours, Joe!" the old sourdough grinned, pulling the whining dog over to the boy's bunk. "Happy birthday!"

"Happy birthday!" Mike Murray echoed, looking at his son and swallowing the lump in his throat.

Joe stared unbelievingly at the long-legged, half-grown dog. Its long, gray fur was tipped black, and its face was sharp and intelligent.

"Thanks, Caribou!" Joe cried out.

"He'll cure what's ailin' you," Caribou Dave said. "If he don't, I'll get you a wolf."

"What's his name?" Joe asked.

"He's got an Indian name a foot long," Caribou Dave grinned. "It means 'Little Dog Who'll Grow Up to Be a Big Dog and Eat Gold Miners for Breakfast.' "

Joe laughed happily. "He looks smart."

"He has to be smart to live in the North," Caribou Dave said. "The Malamute is a dog who never forgets a thing. He's got both a nose and a brain."

"I'll call him Rex," Joe said excitedly. "That's a good name for a dog. Caribou, where did you get him?"

"From some Indians in Dawson City," Caribou Dave said. "I traded two pounds of tea for him."

For the rest of the winter, Dave would have to drink the *cheechako* coffee which he hated. "He's a good dog, but he's got no more manners than a bald-face bear. That's your job, Joe. Teachin' him his manners so he can pull a sled. Begin now."

He walked to the end of the cabin and began clearing it. He rolled a barrel of flour over toward the bunk. Mike Murray helped him empty the corner. Then Caribou Dave hammered a peg hook into the corner directly opposite Joe's bunk. He hammered two other hooks into the moss chinking, one on either side of the center hook.

Through the hooks he slipped three lash ropes and tied them to the puppy's collar. He grabbed the puppy and tied a fourth rope to its tail. Shivering and snarling, the pup bared its teeth.

"Rex, you varmint!" Caribou Dave grinned. "Don't you want Joe to civilize you? Hey, Joe, talk to him."

"Rex, Rex," the boy said softly. "Nobody's going to hurt you. Be a good dog, Rex. Oh, Pop, if Annie could see Rex!" he exclaimed. "I'll write her a letter about Rex!"

Caribou Dave walked to the boy's bunk, the ends of the four ropes in his hands. "This is how you civilize these varmints, Joe. You holler, 'Mush!' and pull the center rope like this. Mush! Mush!" he yelled, tugging on the center rope. He dragged the dog forward until its head rammed into the log wall.

"You're hurting him!" Joe protested.

"He's got a head harder than a rock," Caribou Dave said dryly. "That's what you do when you holler 'Mush!' "

"To make him go left, I pull the left rope?" Joe asked.

"Yes, and you holler, 'Haw!' To make him go right you holler, 'Gee!' To make him walk backwards, you pull this rope here that's tied to his tail, and when you want him to stop you holler, 'Whoa!' That's all there is to it."

Caribou Dave put the ends of the four lash ropes into Joe's hands. "You got to smash those words into his Indian head, Joe."

Whether it was because he had the dog to train or whether it was because his body was naturally strong and was recuperating anyway, Joe began to feel better. He was the first one to awake in the morning. "Rex!" he would whisper to the pup sleeping beside his bunk. "Here, puppy! Here, Rex!"

The dog would push his nose against Joe's hand. It was a cold nose, almost as cold as the icicles in the cabin. Mornings, with the stove dead, the temperature inside was almost as low as it was outside. When the two men awoke, they would light the kerosene stove and start a good fire.

"That boy's as good as new," Caribou Dave said one morning, a week or so after Rex's arrival. "Mike," he joked, "I think Joe ought to get a pick and shovel and help us."

The father stepped over to Joe's bunk and tousled the boy's shaggy long hair. "That Rex'd be better than a fur robe if you could teach him to sleep in the bunk with you," Mike Murray said to his son.

"He doesn't trust me enough to sleep in the bunk," Joe said as he petted the dog's head.

Caribou Dave snorted. "I could rig up a rope and when you hollered, 'Bunk!' and hauled on the rope, he'd come flyin' in!"

They all laughed. The boy was mending, and the gold pans going down into the second prospect hole were promising. "Good luck is like bad luck," Caribou Dave was saying these days. "Never comes by its lonesome."

When Joe was asleep, all the two men could talk about was the second prospect hole.

One afternoon, they rushed into the cabin like two celebrating Chilkoot Indians. Rex snarled and retreated to Joe's bunk where the boy was sitting, the four lash ropes in his hands.

"We hit it!" Joe's father yelled. Digging his hand into his pocket, he tossed what seemed to be five or six bright yellow marbles into the air. They glittered in the light of the lamp as they fell to the floor. "Joe, we hit it!" Mike Murray grinned and began to jig up and down. He sang snatches of song and hollered out war-whoops.

While Mike Murray, the quiet one, jigged and sang like a crazy clown, Caribou Dave picked up the shining yellow lumps from the floor. The old sourdough, always so full of talk and jokes, didn't have a word in him. He studied the nuggets, shaking his head. At last he spoke. "Joe, want to see 'em?"

The dog snarled at both miners. Rex had a white man's name, but he was still an Indian dog, and he didn't understand the white man's gold fever.

"Those nuggets were lyin' in the sand waitin' to be picked up," Caribou Dave said to Joe in the quietest of voices.

"We hit the paystreak!" Mike Murray, the quiet one, roared at the top of his voice. He ran over to Joe and kissed him, breaking away to grab Caribou Dave's hands. The two men, still wearing their parkas, began to dance like a couple of lumbering bears.

Rex leaped into the bunk. Joe put his arm around the dog's shivering head.

"See you later, son," Mike Murray said with a laugh. "Caribou, let's go dig some more nuggets!"

When they had gone Joe gently pushed the dog out of his bunk. He picked up the four lash ropes and said, "Rex, how would you like another lesson? You would? Good dog. We'll have another lesson. Mush!" he called, and with only the slightest of pressures on the mush rope, the dog trotted forward.

The boy didn't have to smash the dog's head into the logs as Caribou Dave had advised.

"Good boy, Rex!" Joe said. "Now we'll try going to the left. Haw! Haw!"

The dog veered to the left and Joe grinned happily. "I feel so good, Rex!" he said.

He went over and hugged the dog. "I feel so good, Rex. Pop and Caribou and everything."

CHAPTER TEN

Deep Dark Winter

THERE was no sunlight now on Gold Creek. One dark day followed another. And always the snow fell, a light, almost invisible snow, a snow like a falling curtain.

Up on the slope Joe was cutting firewood. He rested a minute, leaning on his axe. He could see his dog Rex hitched to the wood-sled. But half the cabins on Gold Creek were blotted out or distorted by the thin, glassy snow.

He loaded up the sled and whistled at Rex. "Mush!" he called.

Trees leaped and twisted before him like living shapes in the ghostly twilight. At the cabin, he piled the firewood against the wall. He walked down to the creek. Two more shapes that Joe knew were his father and Caribou Dave were busy working.

They had broken through the creek ice and shoveled it away. Joe helped them shovel frozen gravel into the open ditch they had chopped out across the creek—the beginnings of a dam. For when winter ended—though it didn't seem as if it ever would!—they had to be ready to wash the gold out of their hill of pay dirt.

The three partners on Six-Above were all working ten and twelve hours a day. And in the eternal darkness, the gold-gravel coming up in the buckets at the second prospect hole no longer excited them. They were too tired. They were always tired.

"The paystreak's about done," Caribou Dave said sleepily one night.

And, sleepily, Mike Murray answered him, "Better sink a third hole."

Both men were silent. They would have to burn and dig their way down again. Maybe they would be lucky, or, as with the first hole, they might find nothing. They yawned and the boy yawned and even the dog Rex yawned.

On some days a muddy twilight glimmered. But at night if the moon was out it was always brighter than the day. The Aurora Borealis waved across the sky, and Joe, looking up at these mysterious northern lights, always felt lonely and homesick.

The Aurora Borealis waved across the sky

Vivid streaks of light would spin out of a single star and spread until the whole sky was a web of color.

Lonely nights, when his father sat dozing over his Bible and Caribou Dave sat reading a tattered old newspaper. One evening the boy picked up a pencil and wrote a letter to his sister Annie:

Gold Creek Camp,
Dawson City, Yukon
Feb. 10, 1898

Dear Sister,

It is always dark now. We all miss the sun, even Rex. The snow is so tiny you cannot see it. It hides things. Today I heard the bells of a dog team. I could not see the dogs. I only heard the bells. It was strange as if they were dog ghosts.

Pop is well and so is Caribou Dave and me. We have sunk a third hole but it is too soon to tell. We all send our love to Mom and Uncle Bill.

Your loving brother,
Joe

He never wrote home about the endless work or the dirty clothes hanging on the nails in the cabin. Or about the mice dirt in the half-empty sacks of flour and beans. "The secret animal of the Klondike is the louse," Caribou Dave used to say. "The secret sign of the Klondike is scratchin'."

Joe never wrote home about frostbite or how the frostbitten skin rubbed off. Or about the wolves that, night after night, howled from the hills. Or the wild shrieks in the timber when the sap in the trees froze, splitting the living wood.

In the morning he would give his letter to a miner going into Dawson City. From there, it would go out to Dyea or Skagway by dog sled at one dollar a letter.

Lonely nights, when he would think of his mother and sister and yet find himself unable to write a letter home. As if the deep, dark winter held his hands fast.

"I'd like to go to Dawson City," Caribou Dave announced one night, tramping into the cabin. He had been over to visit Dratfeld and Mogantte.

"Why don't you go?" Joe's father smiled. "We've got plenty of gold dust in the poke now."

"There's bright lights in Dawson City!" the sourdough said. "There's faro and poker! But I ain't hittin' the trail to Dawson City."

"Why not?" Joe's father asked as the boy listened.

"Dratfeld told me all about his last trip. Said they're all hangin' around without one word to say to each other. All of them homesick. Said the only song those opery singers want to sing is 'Home Sweet Home.' Said it made him feel he was at his own funeral."

"This winter'll be gone soon," Mike Murray said.

"Speakin' of funerals," Caribou Dave said, "Halley, down the creek, took a shot at his partner Dickerson last night. Missed him. And that fool of a Dickerson is still workin' alongside that crazy man!"

"Why did he do that?" Joe exclaimed.

"Why?" Caribou Dave shrugged. "It's a poor claim they got, but that ain't the whole answer. No sun, that's why. The human varmint wasn't made for the Klondike."

"Joe," his father said. "If you see Halley don't argue with him. If you're alone when you see him, you holler for me or Caribou."

"Pop, I've got Rex," Joe said. The dog had put on weight and heft. His gray fur was sleek, and the boy was proud of him.

Caribou Dave walked over to the table and glanced down at the big Bible. "It's worth its weight in gold," he said. "In Dawson City they're readin' old papers till they fall to pieces."

He picked up the Bible and hefted it in his hand. "Weighs four pounds. At sixteen dollars an ounce, that Bible's worth—let me see." He found a pencil and worked out the sum. "One thousand and twenty-four dollars!"

"I wouldn't sell it," Mike said. He smiled, and taking the Bible from Caribou Dave, leafed through the pages. "You think we have it dark. Listen to this." He read:

" 'Now the Lord had prepared a great fish to swallow up Jonah. And Jonah was in the belly of the fish three days and three nights.' "

"Least, Jonah could eat fish and not get scurvy," Caribou Dave said, his eyes twinkling. "This Klondike wouldn't be so bad if there was just a little sun."

CHAPTER ELEVEN

Cleanup

IN MARCH, the miners of Gold Creek began to look for the sun as eagerly as they searched for nuggets. Early each morning, they climbed the gulches and stared hopefully at the snowy-white eastern horizon.

One morning, the sun glowed in the east. The giant nugget of the sun! The crowd of men waved their arms. They shouted!

"The sun! There she is, thank God!"

"Dear sun, dear sun!"

The dogs barked joyously. Caribou Dave turned toward Mike Murray and Joe. There were tears in the sourdough's eyes. "It's the same after every winter," he said, putting one arm around Mike's shoulders and the other about the boy's.

Joe wiped his eyes and patted Rex's head. He

looked at the cheering miners. Their clothes were in rags after the long seven-month winter, their feet bound in blanket strips. The boy was as ragged as any miner present, his blond hair as long as his sister Annie's.

"We'll go home soon," the father said to his son, sighing. "And Caribou'll come with us."

Caribou Dave grunted. "We've got work to do before snivelin' about goin' home."

As the days lengthened, the three partners completed the dam they had started to build across the creek. They built sluices and set them up on trestles below the dam. The sluices were long wooden boxes in which they would wash out the pay dirt once the ice melted and water was available.

On their claim they had piled up two hills of pay dirt and four hills of waste. The first and fourth prospect holes they had sunk were worthless. The second prospect hole had been the bonanza, while the third prospect hole was, in Caribou Dave's words, "a nice little tidy one."

Every day it got a little warmer. Joe could hear the water gurgling under the creek ice. And then one morning the ice broke.

"Winter's over!" Mike Murray said to his son.

"We ought to thank God we're alive and well."

The snow began to vanish. Ferns and grasses appeared. Starwort and fireweed, wild roses and heliotrope blossomed. The birches and alders waved new green leaves among the black spruce. One spring day when Joe was too exhausted to lift a shovel, his father ordered him to go into the hills and rest. The boy had hiked across the moss with Rex at his heels, watching the butterflies and birds flying under the blue sky. The moss he stepped on was as brilliantly colored as a rug, and the boy

wondered if the long Yukon winter had been only a dream.

"Rex," he said to the dog. "You're a winter dog. I got you on my birthday when it was forty below."

But with the cleanup time, there were few holidays. Day after day, Joe toiled with his father and Caribou Dave, shoveling the pay gravel into the sluice boxes.

The boxes were fifteen feet long, a foot high and a foot wide, and one fitted into the other.

"I'm letting the water in," Mike Murray called from the dam.

Joe straightened up and glanced at his father, who now with warm weather had sprouted a dark beard on his jaws and chin. Everybody on Gold Creek was bearded, and the boy secretly wished that he, too, could have grown what Caribou Dave called "weeds" on his chin.

Mike Murray opened the dam gate. The water rushed into the first of the sluice boxes, breaking up the clumps of gravel. A muddy stream ran down the sluice line into the tail race at the end.

"Run, run, run!" Caribou Dave chanted. "Wash out the gold, you water! We waited long enough for you!"

Every twenty minutes or so, they let another stream of water into the sluice boxes. All day long they shoveled in the pay dirt and washed it. The gold was caught on wooden cleats nailed along the bottoms of the sluices. When the water was shut off, the three partners brushed with whisk brooms the mud and gold trapped on the cleats.

"Here's a nice nugget!" Joe cried, picking up a shining nugget for the others to see.

"Work, boy!" Caribou Dave called from his

place lower down on the sluice line. "Work! We'll talk about it tonight."

Up and down the creek on all the claims, the miners labored without let-up. They were like human beavers busy with the water work.

Joe dropped the nugget into a box. He picked up a paddle and lifted the heavy mud from the cleat into his gold pan. Filling the pan with water, he began to rinse it, staring down at the swirling mud in the pan. Now and then he saw a glint of gold.

Mosquitoes buzzed around his head, but he paid no attention to the pests. It took a half hour to wash out a pan. Sometimes Joe was sent to the tail race where there was a quicksilver plate to catch the fine flour gold. The heavy, silver-white quicksilver absorbed the fine particles of gold. Later, they would bake the plate and the gold would come free.

Flour gold and coarse gold and nuggets! The yellow stuff for which every miner on Gold Creek had risked his life and endured seven months of the Klondike winter.

One evening, five or six miners visited the three partners on Six-Above. They sat indoors because the mosquitoes were becoming a terrible nuisance again. There were Dratfeld and Mogantte from the claim below, and Sid Edwards, who had discovered the Gold Creek diggings, and Halley, who had gone mad one winter night and shot at his partner, and a couple of others. They spoke about the battleship *Maine,* blown up in February, and the war with Spain.

But then the talk shifted to the news of Gold Creek, and the outside world seemed as far away as the moon.

"The gold's running heavy on my claim," Dratfeld said. "Frenchy and me are washing a thousand a day. How about you, Caribou?"

"You ask the superintendent!" Caribou Dave jabbed his thumb over at Joe Murray.

The boy looked at the bearded men and grinned shyly. "Our pan today ran about two thousand dollars."

"Joe," Caribou Dave asked solemnly. "What do you figure we'll pan for the winter's work?"

"About sixty thousand for the three of us," Joe said.

"Me and my pard'll feel bad if we don't pan a hundred thousand," Sid Edwards said. "When we hit the outside we're travelin' to New York City by Pullman. We aim to eat at Delmonico's every night and have steak for breakfast."

They all laughed except Halley, who had listened to the talk, silent and glum, pulling nervously at his scraggly brown beard. They all knew that Halley and his partner wouldn't pan five thousand between them for the winter's digging.

"Steak," Halley muttered. "Me and Dickerson'll be lucky to eat oatmeal when we go home."

Mike Murray tried to cheer the man. "You can stake another claim next winter."

"What claim?" Halley asked bitterly. "We were lucky getting on Gold Creek. Least, you men were lucky."

"There'll be other discoveries," Caribou Dave said. "There are hundreds of creeks in this country nobody's put a pan into. The Klondike ain't the last rush by a long shot."

Halley stood up to go. "There's an army of men coming up in June. Three thousand boats, they say."

"Won't you have some coffee?" Mike Murray invited.

But Halley clomped out of the cabin. The miners all glanced at each other. "I wouldn't want to be Dickerson," Caribou Dave remarked.

"I wouldn't want to be Halley," Joe's father said thoughtfully. "He isn't himself. The Klondike winter is still in him."

CHAPTER TWELVE

Miners' Meeting

AT TWILIGHT a few days later, the three partners wearily entered their cabin. Caribou Dave was carrying the sack holding the day's cleanup. He dropped it to the floor. Then he flung himself onto his bunk as if he were another sack.

Mike Murray sat down on a box and lit his pipe. Rex stretched out at Joe's feet.

"Why's that dog behavin' like *he* put in a day's work?" Caribou Dave asked his partners. He yawned. "Might as well put the dust in the bank."

He picked up the heavy cleanup sack of gold dust and walked to an old flour barrel covered with a blanket. They had been depositing the gold dust in this barrel—the "bank," as the old sourdough called it.

Caribou Dave pulled off the blanket. "Either of you touch this blanket?" he asked.

"No," Mike Murray said. "Why?"

"I didn't touch it," Joe said.

Caribou Dave was peering into the barrel. "Somebody's been here," he said slowly. "Somebody's robbed the bank!"

Joe and his father hurried over to him. Inside the barrel, the gold dust shone heavy and yellow. They could see holes in the smooth, flat surface where the dust had been scooped out as if with a tin cup.

"Some dirty crook's took out close to two hundred ounces is my guess!" Caribou Dave said in a voice like chipped ice. "A little more, a little less."

Two hundred ounces! Joe thought. They had been robbed of three thousand dollars!

Caribou Dave walked to the wall where his rifle hung on some nails. "Come on!" he called.

Mike Murray grabbed his rifle. But Joe, rifleless, was following his father to the door when Caribou Dave shouted at him, "Where's your rifle, boy?"

Joe flushed. He hadn't heard Caribou Dave talk to him like this since their hunting trip in the winter. The boy turned and fetched his own rifle.

Outside, the bottle-glass windows in the cabins on Gold Creek gleamed a dusky gold. "Rouse 'em out!" Caribou Dave commanded. "Tell 'em to see to their dust! Tell 'em to come to our cabin for a Miners' Meeting!"

Joe had heard about Miners' Meetings. In Alaska, where there were no Mounties to keep law and order, a Meeting could condemn a man to death if he were convicted of a crime.

"Joe," Caribou Dave said. "You stay in the cabin. Mike, you go up the creek. I'll go down."

"Who could've done it?" Joe asked.

"We'll find out!"

Joe returned to the cabin and sat stiffly on his bunk, his rifle across his knees, Rex at his feet. The dog growled to himself now and then as if he understood that something was wrong.

An hour later a crowd of miners buzzed like mosquitoes outside the Hotel Annie. There were so many of them that Caribou Dave fetched a lamp outside. Joe was bursting with curiosity. He had heard Halley's name mentioned a dozen times. Halley was evidently the thief, but nobody seemed to be angry, not even Caribou Dave.

Joe tugged at his father's elbow. "Pop," he said, "what's it all mean?"

Just then Caribou Dave cried. "I call this Meeting to order!"

The voices quieted and all of them looked toward the cabin where the old sourdough was standing outside the door. The lamp, hanging on a peg, lit up Caribou Dave's solemn, bearded face. "Halley's crazy as a loon," he said, and his voice was solemn too. "Dickerson, you tell 'em!"

Halley's partner walked through the crowd over to Caribou Dave. For some reason he took off his slouch hat before speaking. "Halley's crazy as a loon like Caribou says. Maybe crazier. He stopped working a couple days ago. 'Why should I work?' he says to me. I couldn't reason with him. He was like the time he shot at me in the winter. He kept me awake all night long. 'Why should I work?' he says. He kept muttering, 'Gold, gold!' over and over again. In the morning he seemed better. He said he was going to Dawson City."

"He went to Dawson all right," Caribou Dave said. "Went with a bag of gold! Took two hundred ounces of our dust!"

"And three hundred of ours!" Dratfeld shouted.

"Halley's crazy as a loon," he said

"About fifty of mine that I kept in a tin!" a third miner said.

"Who else has gold missing?" Caribou Dave asked. And when everybody had spoken up, he said, "It comes to somethin' between seven and eight hundred ounces."

"That'd weigh forty or fifty pounds," Mike Murray said.

"Eleven thousand dollars worth of dust!" Dratfeld figured it. "Close to thirteen thousand if it's eight hundred ounces. Well, what are we waiting for? Somebody ought to hit the trail to Dawson City and notify the Mounted Police!"

"Right!" the miners chorused.

"Halley's crazy," his partner Dickerson said. "No telling what he'll do. He didn't take his clothes or grub or nothing. Only his revolver."

"And fifty pounds of dust!" a sarcastic voice lifted out of the crowd. "One of you men who lost dust better hit the trail 'stead of all this powwowing."

"Send the boy!" Dratfeld, who had been robbed of three hundred ounces, shouted. "I can't spare the time!"

"Think *we* can?" Caribou Dave snapped. "It's

"He didn't take his clothes or grub or nothing"

the middle of cleanup for us, too. We've been robbed of two hundred ounces, and I say forget about it! We've got a mountain of pay dirt to wash."

"Then write the Mounties a letter," Dratfeld suggested. "Or next time a gold train goes out, they can notify the Mounties."

"No!" Mike Murray said. "No! Somebody has to go who knows what Halley looks like. The man's crazy and he's got a revolver. He could kill somebody. We're not savages—or maybe we are. Gold savages! I'll send Joe to Dawson City."

The crowd of miners were silent for a second. Then Dratfeld spoke up. "My partner and me, we're the other big loser." He faced Mike Murray and said, "You send the boy and you won't lose by it, Mike. I say this before everybody. If any of that dust is found, my partner and me will give half our share to the boy for his time. If none of it's found, my partner and me will pay the boy a thousand dollars in dust for bringing the warning to Dawson City. Mike Murray is right. We're not savages!"

The crowd cheered and began to disperse to

their cabins. With sunrise, another long day of cleanup lay ahead for all of them.

Mike Murray smiled at his son. "Joe, take some grub and take the dog. You're as good as a man, Joe. That's all I have to say to you."

The boy flushed at his father's praise.

Caribou Dave clapped Joe on the back. "You Murrays are both good men! Not savages like me!"

CHAPTER THIRTEEN

American Mountie

THE trail to Dawson City led through the mining camps on the creeks. It circled the bogs and was muddy most of the way. The sun burned in the sky and there was light sixteen hours a day. Joe only stopped to rest in some miner's cabin when he couldn't push one foot in front of the other.

"You're worn out," a miner told him one evening. "Why don't you try sleeping eight hours?"

"I've explained it to you," the boy said wearily. "Halley's crazy and he's liable to kill somebody. The Mounties have to know just as soon as they can."

"Bub, you talk just like a Mountie," the miner said. He walked to a shelf in his cabin and brought back an orange. "You eat this. It came in on the first steamer from St. Michael."

It was the first orange Joe had seen since he had left Seattle. Looking at the shining golden fruit, he thought of his mother and sister. He thanked the miner and peeled the orange. He thought that people could be real good. His father was right. No man ought to act like a gold savage.

When he arrived in Dawson City, he hurried to Police Headquarters. The redcoated Mountie officer wrote down the information Joe gave him on a big sheet of paper.

"We'll look for Halley," the Mountie said. "I suppose you'll go back to Gold Creek right away?"

"Yes," Joe answered. "They need me."

The Mountie glanced at the tired boy in front of his desk and then at Rex, who was sitting on the floor scratching himself with a lazy paw. "I know," the Mountie said. "Summer cleanup."

He picked up the sheet of paper and read: " 'Robert Halley. Hair and beard dark brown. Eyes dark brown. About forty-five years of age. Weight about one hundred and seventy pounds. Height about five foot ten inches. No scars. No mutilations.' "

The Mountie smiled and said, "That description fits half the men in Dawson, and there are thousands of them. You could help us find Halley if you stayed in town awhile. I hate to ask a favor like this in the middle of summer cleanup. I ask it only because the man is dangerous."

Joe was silent. He wondered what his father would have said if he had been here. As if there were any doubt! "I'll help you," the boy said.

"Thanks," the Mountie said. "You can stay in our barracks unless you're a Klondike millionaire," he joked. "A bed in a good hotel costs ten dollars. A steak is six dollars."

The Mountie was smiling and Joe smiled, too. "Thanks, I'll stay in your barracks."

When he walked out on Front Street, he left the dog behind. The Mountie had said, "You'll be looking for Halley in the saloons, and some of those saloons are so fancy they won't let you inside with a dog."

It was a bright, hot June day. The sun glittered on the broad Yukon where the boats and rafts of the 1898 stampeders lined the shore. There were wooden sidewalks on Front Street this year, but they were so crowded with the new gold-rushers that hundreds walked in the gutter. Dog carts and horse-drawn wagons moved slowly through the

There was no telling a millionaire from a mucker

press of men. *Cheechakos* without a red cent in their pockets. And sourdoughs who had finished their cleanup and sold out their claims.

Everywhere there were banners advertising the arrival and departure of steamships. Music blared out of saloons and dance halls. Dawson City looked as if a circus had just arrived—there were so many idlers. Joe thought that the Mountie was right. Half of those men could have been Halley. In their slouch hats and gumboots, everybody looked alike. There was no telling a millionaire from a mucker.

The boy glanced at the row of buildings on the east side of Front Street. Perhaps Halley was in one of them this very second, spending the stolen gold dust. Joe looked longingly at the tundra sloping up to the mountains. He wished he was back on Gold Creek with his father and Caribou Dave.

There were so many saloons, he thought. The Dominion! The Northern! The Pioneer! The Monte Carlo!

He hesitated and then walked into the Dominion. The boy stopped inside the door, confused. So many faces! Miners were lined up at the bar on the left-hand side of the house where white-aproned bartenders were serving drinks or weigh-

Half of those men could have been Halley

ing the dust they received in payment on their gold scales. The spick-and-span bartenders seemed to be the rich men, but it was the dirty, ragged miners who carried the fat pokes of gold dust.

Over on the right side, another crowd of miners were gambling. There was a faro bank, and stud and draw poker. Perched above the tables, like hawks in their nests, were the lookouts. They were armed with rifles, and their sharp eyes were concentrated on the players below them to see that the house didn't lose any money through carelessness or trickery.

The boy thought that he better begin somewhere. He walked down along the bar, peering at the faces. Voices seemed to dart at him as he passed.

"No man on the Eldorado'll sell for less than a thousand dollars a foot—"

"This man Bruceth washed out sixty-one thousand in gold in one day—"

"I'm gettin' out next week—"

But all the dark-bearded faces in the Dominion were the faces of strangers. Joe tried another place. Now and then his heart jumped for he thought he recognized Halley. But on a second look it turned out to be another stranger.

He was walking among the poker tables at the Monte Carlo when a voice cried out, "Joe Murray!"

Joe paused and stared at Diamond Jack Munson, who was dealing at one of the tables. Diamond Jack's blue eyes were foxy-sharp as ever, his black mustache glossy. His fawn-colored vest was crossed by a huge gold watch chain, and in his green cravat a diamond pin shone.

"Did you strike it rich?" Diamond Jack asked as he dealt the cards to the players. "How was that Chilkoot Pass, Joe?"

The boy didn't answer. He was happy to see Diamond Jack again, but all his weariness of a sudden seemed to weigh him down. The long days on the trail! The thousands of strange faces!

The foxy blue eyes narrowed. "You in trouble, Joe?"

"No," the boy said. "It's not real trouble—"

"Gentlemen," Diamond Jack said to the miners at his table, "please excuse me. That young feller there is the son of the King of France and we noblemen must stick together."

The miners laughed. Diamond Jack spoke to the manager and another dealer took his place.

"Joe," Diamond Jack said, "you don't look so good." He studied the boy's gaunt young face. He saw the long Klondike winter in the boy's hollow cheeks. He felt Joe's arm muscle as he had on the ship to Dyea. "You haven't been digging daisies," he grinned. "Speak up! You broke?"

"No," Joe said. "Pop and me got a good claim on Gold Creek—"

"I don't believe you."

Joe dug his hand into his pocket and pulled out his moosehide poke. Its sides bulged fatly.

"You've got town dust," Diamond Jack admitted. "What's bothering you, Joe?"

He led Joe out onto Front Street and there Joe blurted out the whole story. Diamond Jack thought it over and then he said, "Never can say what a crazy man'll do. Halley might go home. He might bury the dust he stole like a dog burying a bone. He might spend it all. These saloons are open twenty-four hours, Joe. You can't be parading in and out of them. You need a rest, Joe. I can tip off the bartenders and dealers at the Monte

Carlo to keep an eye open for Halley. And I'll tip off the boys in the other places."

"Thanks," Joe said gratefully. "You're always helping me, Jack."

"I'm helping myself," the gambler retorted. "I don't want a crazy man sitting down to my game one of these nights. Helping myself—that's my motto!"

When Joe returned to Police Headquarters and told the Mounties about Diamond Jack's plan to recruit Dawson City's bartenders and card dealers to watch out for Halley, there was laughter.

"Next thing will be to get the dogs to help us keep law and order," one of them joked.

Joe slept in the Mountie barracks, his dog Rex curled up at his feet. In the morning, after breakfast, he again scouted Front Street. It was only seven o'clock, but the crowds loafing everywhere seemed as if they had never gone to sleep. These summer days, the sun sank at half past ten and was up an hour or so after midnight.

Faces! Front Street was a street of faces!

The boy glanced at the smiling, carefree faces of sourdoughs waiting for a river boat to take them fifteen hundred miles down the Yukon to St. Michael. He peered at the grumbling faces of newly arrived *cheechakos*. He glanced at every dark-haired man he passed, but he didn't see Halley.

He looked at the faces of the men walking by Dawson City's two banks, the British North America, which did business in a tent, and the small cabin that was the Canadian Bank of Commerce. Later in the morning, he spoke to Diamond Jack.

"Joe," the gambler said, "tomorrow you want to be down on the river. Swiftwater Bill's expected, and Halley might be in the crowd."

"Who's Swiftwater Bill?" Joe asked.

"Bet you never heard that McKinley's President," Diamond Jack grinned. "Ah, innocent youth! Swiftwater Bill owns half of the Monte Carlo. He went outside last winter to bring in supplies. You be down on the river tomorrow."

The next day, Dawson City more than ever looked like a carnival town. It seemed everyone had flocked to the waterfront. Joe wandered along the fringes of the crowd, searching for Halley.

Suddenly there were loud cheers. Joe stood up on tiptoe. A big canoe was coming up the river. In its prow sat a man who looked very important.

The man wore a Prince Albert coat and a high silk hat. He had a black mustache and he was beaming as he held his arms out in greeting.

The sun shone on the black silk hat of Swiftwater Bill Gates. Behind his canoe, a scow followed, loaded with supplies.

The crowd roared but Joe was no longer looking out on the river. His eyes had fixed on a man in the crowd who was waving his hat, a dark-haired, clean-shaven man. The boy's heart fluttered. Could this man be Halley? Halley without a beard!

Swiftwater Bill stepped ashore. The crowd followed him over toward the Monte Carlo. The man Joe had been watching clapped his hat down on his head and shambled along in the impromptu parade. Joe followed him. He had seen Halley three or four times at most. Was this man Halley?

He slipped closer to the clean-shaven man and shouted, "Halley!"

The man whirled around, his dark eyes blazing, his right hand swinging behind him.

He's reaching for that revolver of his, Joe thought in panic. And then, no longer thinking, he plunged forward, grappling with the crazed man and shouting, "Help! Help!"

CHAPTER FOURTEEN

The Outside

"WE'RE going to celebrate July Fourth in Dawson City," Mike Murray had promised Joe after his return to Gold Creek. "And then we'll go home on the first steamer out."

The three partners were in Dawson City two days before the Fourth. They walked up Front Street, Rex at Joe's heels. Caribou Dave pointed at the bright flags hanging over the hotels and stores and saloons. "All those flags must be up in honor of Joe," he said to Mike. "Joe Murray, the hero of the battle of Halley."

Joe laughed. It seemed a thousand years ago since he had grabbed Halley and stopped him from using his revolver. Miners had rushed in to help him and a Mountie had taken the insane man's gun. At Police Headquarters Halley had blurted out an insane man's confession. The Klondike owed him the gold, Halley had said.

The sack of stolen gold dust was found, minus a few thousand dollars that Halley had spent or gambled.

It was all over now. As Joe looked at the Stars and Stripes and Union Jacks, he felt light-hearted and happy. It was all over, the fourteen-hour days of the cleanup time. The long, dark winter with its sickness and unending gloom. The heartaches and disappointments that had begun at Dyea beach and continued without let-up like an Arctic blizzard. In a few days they would be going outside. Home!

The three partners had left their gear in a hotel. Their gold dust was safe in a bank. Front Street was as muddy as ever, but they paid no attention to the mud. It was as if there had never been any mud.

"Let's get rid of our whiskers," Mike Murray said to Caribou Dave. "Joe can use a scissors himself."

They went into one of the tent barbershops. The beards of the two men were clipped off, their jaws and chins shaven clean. On a chair next to his father, Joe sat and watched his long blond hair drop to the floor.

"Perfume!" Caribou Dave ordered. "We want to smell sweet."

When they left the barbershop, Caribou Dave fingered his torn shirt. "How about some decent clothes?" he asked.

"Prices are high here," Mike Murray said.

"That's what I like!" Caribou Dave grinned. "High prices!"

"Joe," his father said, "this man talks like a Klondike millionaire!"

"We're worth close to thirty thousand dollars a man," Caribou Dave said. "We still own Six-Above. We ain't exactly paupers, Mike."

"Half of what Joe and I made goes to his uncle Bill for staking us," Mike Murray said. "I'm not wasting what we made. I want to build a house for my family when I get home. And Joe and his sister Annie are going to college."

"College!" Caribou Dave groaned. "You going to spoil a sourdough like Joe by sendin' him to college?"

"I want to go," Joe smiled. "And if I go, Annie'll go."

"I want to eat," Caribou Dave said. "Partners, let's eat the best meal money can buy!"

They entered the Arcade Restaurant and when they were seated, they ordered three extra large porterhouse steaks at ten dollars a steak. When Caribou Dave saw a waiter bringing a green cucumber on a plate over to another customer, he yelled to the waiter and asked, "How much is a cucumber?"

"Five dollars for a large one," the waiter said.

"Bring me a large one," Caribou Dave said grandly and winked at Mike Murray and Joe. "I'll give you boys a small bite each."

But when the cucumber came he cut it up into three equal parts. "You're the best partners a man could ever have," he said quietly. "Boys, I been thinkin' it over. I'm not goin' outside with you. Might as well know it right here and now."

Mike Murray and Joe couldn't change his mind. "I belong up here in the north," Caribou Dave said with finality.

His decision saddened the two Murrays. When they left the restaurant, the day seemed to have lost its brightness.

They had left Rex outside and Joe tossed the dog the scraps of their porterhouse steaks. Rex wolfed the meat scraps and gristle. Caribou Dave

"I belong up here in the north,"
Caribou Dave said

smiled. "That dog don't believe in tastin' his grub one bit."

"Caribou," Joe said, "come home with us!"

"Never mind that!" the old sourdough retorted. "Let's go see this Diamond Jack friend of yours."

At the Monte Carlo, Joe introduced Caribou Dave to Diamond Jack Munson, who shook hands all around.

"I'm glad you boys struck it rich," he said, waving his hand at the miners sitting at the poker table. "These men struck it rich, too. But me, I'd rather get my gold out of their sacks than out of the ground."

"You're not getting any of our gold," Mike Murray said. "We're taking it outside."

"I swore off gamblin'," Caribou Dave said. "Lost two fortunes at cards. That's enough."

They arranged to have supper with Diamond Jack that night and again strolled out to Front Street. Mike Murray bought two steamship tickets for Joe and himself. Then they returned to their hotel and rested. They had supper with Diamond Jack and afterwards went to a vaudeville show. The band played the "Blue Danube Waltz," and there were jugglers and dancers and singers. Joe enjoyed himself, but every once in a while he remembered that, on July 6th, he and his father would be leaving Caribou Dave and the Klondike, maybe forever.

Daylight burned twenty hours a day, but for the boy, the hours rushed by swift as the White Horse Rapids on the trail out of Dyea. On the night before the Fourth, he was shocked out of sleep by a pistol shot. Joe sprang out of his bed in the hotel room he shared with his father and Caribou Dave. He dashed to the window and stared down on Front Street. Miners were pouring out of the saloons.

"Hooray for July Fourth!" they hollered.

Pistols and rifles exploded everywhere in Dawson City.

"Let's go down and celebrate!" Caribou Dave said.

It was one celebration after another. On the Fourth, the three partners went to a ball game between two teams that called themselves the Sourdoughs and the Cheechakos. Since there was no baseball equipment in Dawson City, the teams used balls carved out of old boat masts, and for bats, great unwieldy clubs.

"You'll never again see a ball game like this one," Caribou Dave said to Joe. "By next summer Dawson City'll be civilized!"

"Why don't you come home with us?" Joe asked. "I've written my sister Annie about you, Caribou. She's waiting to see you."

The old sourdough's gray-blue eyes gazed steadily into the boy's earnest face. He didn't answer Joe. He only patted his shoulder. Joe looked away and with dim eyes peered at the Cheechako pitcher winding up, a wooden baseball in his fist.

And when Joe stood next to his father on the deck of the steamer that would take them to St. Michael, his eyes were cloudy again. For down on the dock in the noisy crowd, Caribou Dave was waving his slouch hat. And next to the sourdough was Diamond Jack.

The steamer tooted. The crowd on the dock called their last farewells. "Good-by, Mike, Joe!" Caribou Dave shouted. "Good-by! I'm goin' to miss you, Joe."

"Good-by!" Diamond Jack called.

Joe waved at them with tears in his eyes. The figures of the old sourdough and the gambler grew smaller and smaller. And still the boy waved while

He had become a man, a sourdough

Rex next to him snarled out his own Malamute farewell.

The steamer curved around a bend of the Yukon River, and Dawson City was gone.

The smoke from its hillside tents and waterfront hotels drifted up into the blue sky. Mike's arm circled his son's shoulders. "We're going outside at last, Joe. We'll see our family soon. Wipe your tears, son. It was a great experience and you'll never forget it as long as you live. Not any of it. The good and the bad. Caribou Dave and Diamond Jack and all the rest. Even that crazy man Halley. Wipe your tears, Joe. That's what you want to think of. You've seen it all yourself. It's in your heart and you'll never forget it."

It was a long speech for quiet Mike Murray. The boy kept nodding as his father spoke. His eyes cleared and were no longer dim. He stared at the hills, behind which lay Dawson City and the gold creeks of the Klondike.

He felt older than his fifteen years, as if finally he had become a man—a sourdough.

About the Author

BENJAMIN APPEL is one of those rare persons—a native New Yorker. He attended Lafayette College and Columbia University. After college he traveled widely all over the United States and Mexico. During and after World War II he traveled on government missions to the Philippine Islands, Japan, and China. He has logged in Idaho and hunted gold in California. He also has written numerous adult novels and magazine articles, and several of his short stories have been included in the O'Brien and O. Henry collections. He now lives in Roosevelt, New Jersey, and once in a while finds time to go fishing.

About the Artist

IRV DOCKTOR was born in Philadelphia, Pennsylvania, and won a scholarship to the Philadelphia Museum School of Industrial Art. Afterwards, he traveled all over the United States and later, during the war, went to New Zealand, Australia, and Japan. His illustrations have appeared in many leading magazines and in a growing number of books.

About the Historical Consultant

COLONEL HENRY W. CLARK, U.S.A.R., a native of Alaska, has had a remarkably varied career. He has served with distinction in many academic and governmental posts since his early fame as Harvard's Phi Beta Kappa All-American football player during the 1920's. Formerly professor of history at Lafayette University, he served as an army colonel during World War II and, during the postwar years, as general manager of the Alaska Development Board. He is the author of A HISTORY OF ALASKA and ALASKA, THE LAST FRONTIER.

WE WERE THERE BOOKS

1. WE WERE THERE ON THE OREGON TRAIL
   By WILLIAM O. STEELE. Historical Consultant: PROFESSOR RAY W. IRWIN. *Illustrated by* JO POLSENO
2. WE WERE THERE AT THE BATTLE OF GETTYSBURG
   By ALIDA SIMS MALKUS. Historical Consultant: EARL S. MIERS. *Illustrated by* LEONARD VOSBURGH
3. WE WERE THERE AT THE BOSTON TEA PARTY
   By ROBERT N. WEBB. Historical Consultant: PROFESSOR LOUIS L. SNYDER. *Illustrated by* E. F. WARD
4. WE WERE THERE WITH BYRD AT THE SOUTH POLE
   By CHARLES S. STRONG. Historical Consultant: COLONEL BERNT BALCHEN, U.S.A.F. *Illustrated by* GRAHAM KAYE
5. WE WERE THERE AT THE NORMANDY INVASION
   By CLAYTON KNIGHT. Historical Consultant: MAJOR GENERAL RALPH ROYCE, U.S.A.F., RETIRED. *Illustrated by the Author*
6. WE WERE THERE IN THE KLONDIKE GOLD RUSH
   By BENJAMIN APPEL. Historical Consultant: COLONEL HENRY W. CLARK, U.S.A., RETIRED. *Illustrated by* IRV DOCKTOR
7. WE WERE THERE WITH THE MAYFLOWER PILGRIMS
   By ROBERT N. WEBB. Historical Consultant: GEORGE F. WILLISON. *Illustrated by* CHARLES ANDRES
8. WE WERE THERE WITH THE PONY EXPRESS
   By WILLIAM O. STEELE. Historical Consultant: SYLVESTER VIGILANTE. *Illustrated by* FRANK VAUGHN
9. WE WERE THERE WITH THE CALIFORNIA FORTY-NINERS
   By STEPHEN HOLT. Historical Consultant: OSCAR LEWIS. *Illustrated by* RAYMOND LUFKIN
10. WE WERE THERE WITH ETHAN ALLEN AND THE GREEN MOUNTAIN BOYS
    By ROBERT N. WEBB. Historical Consultant: CHILTON WILLIAMSON. *Illustrated by* ROBERT PIOUS

In Preparation

11. WE WERE THERE WITH JEAN LAFITTE AT NEW ORLEANS
    By IRIS VINTON. *Illustrated by* ROBERT GLAUBKE
12. WE WERE THERE AT THE OKLAHOMA LAND RUN
    By JIM KJELGAARD. *Illustrated by* CHRIS A. KENYON, JR.

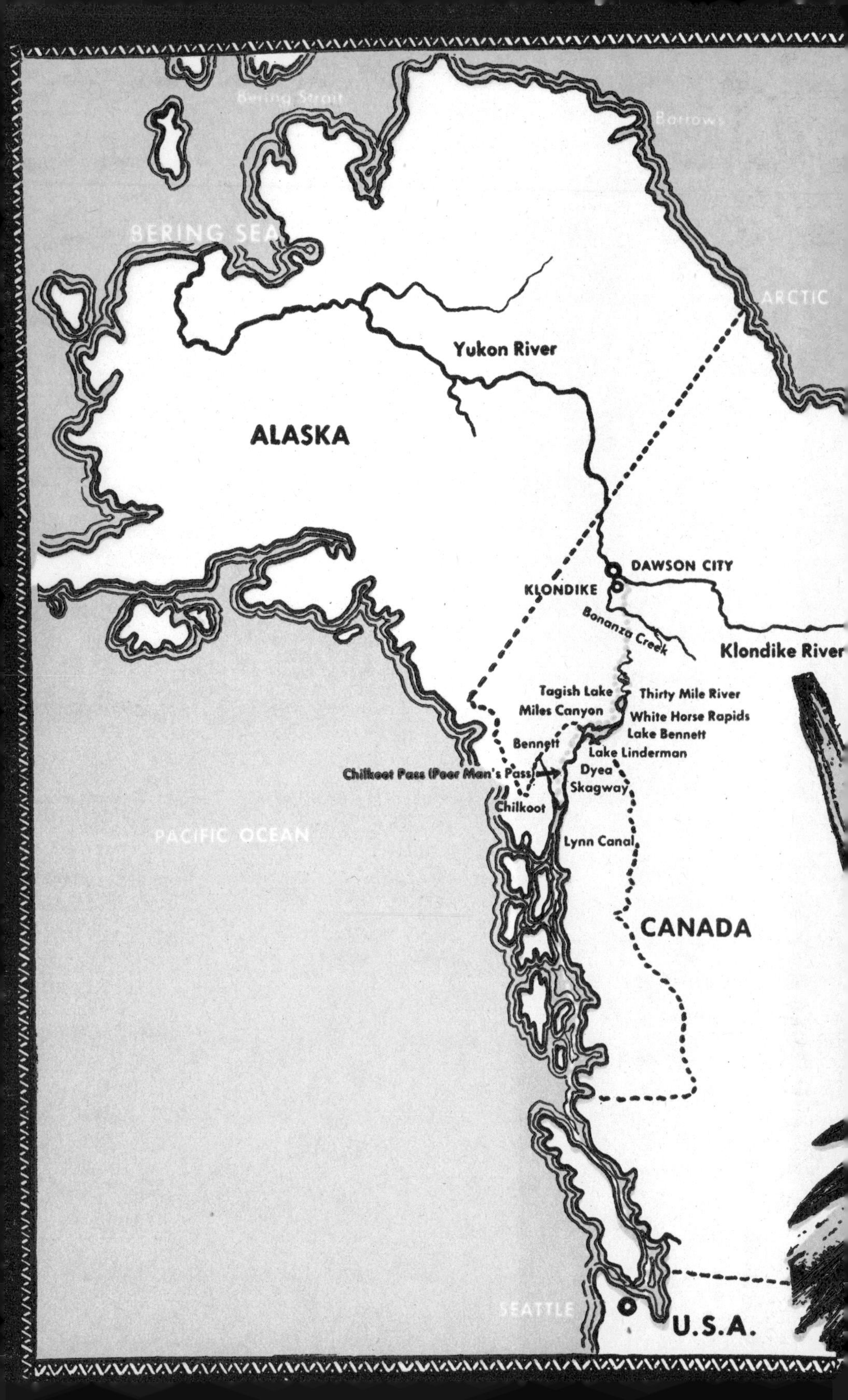

Bering Strait
Barrows
BERING SEA
ARCTIC
Yukon River
ALASKA
DAWSON CITY
KLONDIKE
Bonanza Creek
Klondike River
Tagish Lake
Thirty Mile River
Miles Canyon
White Horse Rapids
Lake Bennett
Bennett
Lake Linderman
Chilkoot Pass (Poor Man's Pass)
Dyea
Skagway
Chilkoot
PACIFIC OCEAN
Lynn Canal
CANADA
SEATTLE
U.S.A.